SPEAK NO EVIL

SPEAK NO EVIL

GRANT GRIFFIN

SPEAK NO EVIL

Edited by Becca James
Cover Art by Taylor Goins-Phillips

iUniverse books may be ordered through booksellers or by contacting:

iUniverse
1663 Liberty Drive
Bloomington, IN 47403
www.iuniverse.com
844-349-9409

ISBN: 978-1-6632-0637-4 (sc)
ISBN: 978-1-6632-0636-7 (e)

Library of Congress Control Number: 2020914380

Print information available on the last page.

iUniverse rev. date: 08/20/2020

Dedicated to my sister, Janna Danae "Butt Head" Rhodes.
Thank you for making me so angry that I threatened to sew that
big, fat mouth shut. This book would not exist without you.
I love you, Skippy.

CONTENTS

PROLOGUE

Howdy-doo, reader? Yes, you, the one who cracked open the weird book with the demented scarecrow on the cover reading this in your comfy arm chair while sipping on a glass of Lipton Peach Iced Tea. I'm talking to you through a book. Isn't that neat? I would like to personally thank you for picking up my manuscript. You are single-handedly keeping my spice garden afloat and my capuchins well-fed, and if Momo and Pepe could speak or write forewords for that matter, they would kiss your feet and probably those sweet, supple cheeks of yours. I'm getting off topic.

Listen up and listen well. I don't want to hear about any of you chuckleheads running around thinking choices don't matter. In this universe (you heard that right, *this universe*) the world could change based on whether or not a fly broke wind on my chili dog. Only certain people in the universe get the opportunity to see all the choices laid out before them, like reading the panels of a comic book or the synopsis of a novel. We may come from different worlds, but believe it when I say that your choices matter, and they affect everyone around you in ways that you are either too selfish or too unaware to realize. Just like the select few in this universe, you have the power to change your reality for the good of yourself and everyone around you. You just don't know it yet. If we really are made in God's image, think of what latent abilities He has given us and how we could wield them to treat others better and fulfill that truth.

Anyway, I hope you enjoy my book. Have fun, take your time, don't dog ear the pages, *pay attention to everything,* and remember, your choices matter. Good or bad, they can change everything. Y'all have a good day now!

Grant Griffin **A B C D E F G H I J K L M N O P Q R S T U V W X Y Z 10 A=J**

A NEEDLE PULLING THREAD

"Kill you with the sword? Jesus, Stone. Have you ever seen anything like this?" Detective Leroy Stone stood unblinking and unfazed at the constant flashing of a camera and the hideous tableau before him. Terrified unblinking eyes stared back in return with a visage bloodied and marred by the torture of a madman with a penchant for pain and suffering. The victim was awake the whole time the surgery and stitches were administered. Leroy shuddered at the idea that this could be described using medical jargon. Maybe it was a way to distance himself from the horror that laid before him.

His name was Ezra Wisneski. He was a local apartment tycoon-turned-politician that was currently running for mayor of Little Heaven. He owned three complexes, if you could even call them that, and they were all named after him and a body of water that did not exist in or around the complex. The bigger the body of water, the more run down and decrepit the apartments were, the locals would say.

The man was well-dressed, covered with Dolce & Gabbana fabrics from head to toe. Leroy would have to work overtime for three months to be able to afford his shoes alone. That's one of the perks when you're a slumlord in a city of almost 15,000 people. It's not like the fancy clothes and steady paychecks saved him in the end. Leroy was sure that he begged for his life, that he bribed his killer, and that he said he would never do whatever he did to deserve this again. What he couldn't tell, however, was if the psycho sewed this victim's mouth shut so he would stop begging or if it was a part of the sick punishment he felt the crooked businessman was owed.

Talk is cheap when words have no value, Leroy said to himself. *Just like Jacob used to say.* His eyes rested on the mouth, the thick black string piercing skin and opening up holes in the victim's lips, the blood dried from finally seeing the open air.

"Stone? Stone! Detective Leroy Daniel Stone! Daniel, for Christ's sake, talk to me!" The gruff, cigarette-addled voice of Little Heaven Police Commissioner Marleen Stricker punctured through Leroy's thought process. He scowled at the woman, offended that she used his full name to get his attention and, worse, his middle name.

"I told you! It's Leroy or Detective Stone, Commissioner." Leroy's eyes immediately settled back onto the corpse duct taped to the wall.

"And I told you, it's Marleen or nothing," the commissioner shot back, amused that she annoyed him enough to get his attention. "What else was I supposed to do? You went all Stone Mode on me, and I did not know how to break through."

Leroy rolled his eyes, and Marleen gave him a friendly punch on the shoulder.

"Aw, c'mon. Don't be like that now. I'm just glad to work with you again. It's been a while since we collaborated like this. Makes me think of the old times."

"You and I both know those days are long gone, Commissioner," Leroy said, still examining the body. "What were you saying anyway? I was thinking."

Marleen stood to Leroy's left, finally taking the time to absorb the image on the wall instead of walking down memory lane.

"I asked if you've seen anything like this. I mean, Little Heaven has its problems, but a psycho killer was never one of them."

Leroy grunted in agreement. He and Marleen had been on the force for almost two decades this year. The sleepy oil town that was Little Heaven, Georgia had its fair share of drugs, gang activity, and dirty cops, but a murder like this was entirely new.

"So we have someone who knows how to sew and more than likely believes that what they are doing is right. That certainly narrows it down.

Is it too early to say that this is a serial killer?" Marleen asked. The idea of telling the press that the frontrunner for the mayor's office was viciously killed with a myriad of cryptic words painted around the outline of the lifeless pinned-up body did not seem like a walk in the park to any parties involved.

"Far too early. And keep the press out of it. Tell them Wisneski's gone missing and we are working our hardest to find him. If those vultures get ahold of this freak show, the GBI will get involved and they're gonna turn whoever this is into the next Wayne Williams."

"Williams wasn't a visionary killer. You know there's no way that we can keep this quiet."

"They're better off not knowing," Leroy said, running his gloved hand across the wall supporting the victim. The message written around his body was in bold, capitalized letters, and it promised death to those who stepped out of this psychopath's code of conduct.

YOU SHALL NOT MISTREAT ANY WIDOW OR FATHERLESS CHILD. MY WRATH WILL BURN, AND I WILL KILL YOU WITH THE SWORD.

Leroy tore himself away from the confusing message to examine the rest of the room. The abandoned home Wisneski was found was on the cops' radar when a package was sent to the admissions office of his complex. The poor office manager decided to open up said package, and to her surprise, sitting on a bed of ice was a bloody human tongue. The proper authorities were immediately identified, and the return address on the package led the police to the abandoned home. It was on the outskirts of Little Heaven, about fifty miles from Chaytonville. The owner of the house had been long dead, and this whole neighborhood was about to be paved over so new unoriginal houses could be crammed together in its place. Leroy imagined that the value of this neighborhood went down by at least a good 50,000 per home now that it was the site of a grisly murder.

"So who do you think the message is for?"

Leroy glanced over at the dark, red letters bordering the victim. He scanned the inscription from top to bottom, muttering to himself as his eyes moved back and forth.

"He could be telling us why he killed Wisneski. Maybe he's a religious zealot trying to start the apocalypse, or maybe he's just insane. Who knows right now?"

"Is that a legitimate lead, or are you simply spewing bullcrap? You are the best detective I have, Stone. I need you in this case."

"Pass." Leroy said, dismissively throwing a hand up. "Give it to some bright-eyed meter maid looking to become the next commissioner."

Marleen scoffed at Leroy's comment. "Ouch, thanks. You knew that the commissioner's job was yours, but threw it away without even considering. I would have been happy to work under you, but you *hadn't* and *haven't* gotten over what happened to Jacob."

Before Leroy could fire back at his oldest friend, the CSI photographer stopped to take a break and check a notification on his phone. The young man's eyes grew wide as he ran over to where Marleen and Leroy were arguing.

"Excuse me, Commissioner," the young man said in between breaths. "You're gonna want to take a look at this."

Marleen took the photographer's phone to see a red-haired anchorwoman delivering breaking news on the local station WRFD.

"We interrupt this program to give you startling news of a video that we just received at the studio. An unidentified person calling himself The Seamstress is apparently admitting to committing the murder of mayoral candidate Ezra Wisneski. He is also addressing the citizens of Little Heaven. We recommend that you remove any children in the room."

The feed of the news anchor cut to a murky room with a table and a solitary light bulb above the table. A person covered from head to toe in a black winter jacket and gloves was sitting down, a hood covering his face. As the figure slowly looked up at the camera, the sliver of light above him revealed a mask constructed from a myriad of cloth with two buttons for eyes, one red and one blue. What sent shivers down Leroy's spine was the smile. It was a smile that reflected the victim's threaded fate, matted with dried blood and all. He looked like a deranged scarecrow, a nightmare out of the minds of children who read too many Stephen King novels at too early of an age. The Seamstress sat silently, the red and blue button eyes staring into the 14,756 souls of the sleepy Georgia town.

"Good evening, citizens of Little Heaven," he began in a low and garbled voice. "I want to start off by saying I do not kill without a purpose. Most of you know the power of words and how something as innocuous as a newspaper article can destroy a life. You may also be wondering who is speaking to you, but that does not matter. What matters is what I say next. And what I am going to say is very important." The video skipped to a clip of Wisneski tied to a chair, begging and pleading for his life. Though he remained on the screen, his wailing and sputtering were muted and replaced by the killer's horrific voiceover.

"Most of you know charismatic mayoral candidate and unforgiving slumlord Ezra Wisneski. Subsidized by oil and and the very lives of the less fortunate. Two days ago, I severed his silver tongue and sewed his acid-spitting mouth shut forever."

Wisneski squirmed with twice the intensity when the masked figure appeared in the frame of the video and pulled out a butcher knife. As the murderer's body eclipsed the camera lens, all that could be heard was Ezra's blood-curdling cry, a scream so deeply disturbing that even someone as seasoned as Leroy and Marleen winced at the sound of it.

Static broke up the sickening display before the grisly masked man sitting at the table blurred back into view. "Mr. Wisneski stole the homes of women without husbands and children without fathers, and now, his children have no father and his wife has no husband. Ezra Wisneski was a fork-tongued devil, and I will shut the mouths of every fork-tongued devil I can find. I will baptize every devil in Little Heaven with oil and set their corpses aflame so they understand the hell that's waiting for them."

Once more, the screen transitioned, this time to Wisneski's body hanging upside down, his eyes wide open and his stitched up mouth dripping with fresh blood. "I am The Seamstress, and those who use their words to destroy will die by my hand. I have said, and now I shall do."

No sooner than the warning was uttered, the video abruptly dissolved to a black screen with the address of where the body had been found in white letters. Immediately, WRFD switched back to the news anchor, who began repeating what was shared for those just tuning in.

Leroy and Marleen had been watching the unpleasant spectacle without so much as a peep. They both slowly turned to look at one another, their eyes filled with worry and terror.

"Still think this is Little Heaven's Wayne Williams?" Marleen queried, breaking the silence.

Leroy glanced back at what used to be Ezra Wisneski, the bloody, stringy smirk still sending chills up his spine despite the ten feet that separated him from the corpse. He deeply inhaled, refusing to look at Marleen, eyes now fixated on those words: *AND I WILL KILL YOU WITH THE SWORD.*

"No," Leroy suddenly said. "This is worse. So much worse."

CQN

II

A COUPLE JUST CAUSES

Simone Garcia, investigative reporter for *The Trumpet of Heaven,* sped down St. Matthew Drive in her blue 1998 Volvo, swearing at cars who got in her way in a mixture of English and Spanish. She only had a small window of opportunity to get this exclusive. At least, that's what she explained to her editor-in-chief not even twenty minutes ago when she barged into his office with a video of some wacko called The Seamstress. His office was the biggest in the building, full of books, memorabilia from classic movies, like *The Thing, Star Wars: The Empire Strikes Back,* and, to the surprise of many people in the office, *Hairspray.* Gabriel never felt the need to defend anything he bought, and Simone respected him for that.

"I dunno, Jaws. Even for you, I think this is way too high-profile."

Simone smiled at Gabriel Tacey's nickname for her. Jaws. She had a reputation of chasing down stories, and if someone did her city wrong, she would tear them apart on the front page of *The Trumpet.* However, Simone was told for the past few years to stay away from any crime stories and, instead, wrote puffery about the newest bakery on Beach Street or profiles of men like Ezra Wisneski and Clarke Holt, the Chief Executive Officer of Holt Oil Company. Although she could admit that HoltCo had kept Little Heaven from going under, Clarke Holt was a greedy and selfish man, and the fact that he was Ezra Wisneski's biggest supporter, financially and otherwise, definitely cast a bad light on Wisneski as well. Either way, someone as dedicated to finding the truth as Simone "Jaws" Garcia could never be trusted with a measly character profile.

More often than not, her interviews with men like this turned into what Gabriel called "a swim in the shark tank." Because these men were best buddies with Micheal Locklear, the new owner of *The Trumpet*, they expected nice interviews about where they liked to eat or what songs comprised their Spotify playlist. Instead, they were treated with queries of matters they would rather not discuss with someone with a reputation like Simone Garcia. She was not afraid of these men, and she was certainly not afraid of Micheal Locklear. She was going to tell the truth even if these men never saw justice. Today, however, someone had listened and brought justice upon Ezra Wisneski. Permanently.

"Come on, Gabe. You know Locklear wants me off the character profiles. This could be my next big break. I wrote the story about Wisneski evicting 100 people. I should follow up on this, too."

"Your next big break, huh?" Gabriel turned around from staring out his office window. He was a tall, well-groomed man with a full beard and closely-trimmed hair. His large, strong arms leaned against his desk toward Simone. It was riddled with memorabilia as well. On his left was a vintage record single of "ELO Boys" by Cheap Trick, and on his right were three leather-bound Bibles. Each had three letters on the spine: ESV. It was the only version of the Bible that Gabriel would ever read.

Simone would never tell him this, but Gabriel was the only one who could get to her. She instinctively swallowed nervously when he leaned forward. He was the closest thing to a father figure she had since her father passed away. Considering that he also started *The Trumpet* out of his garage, he definitely was someone to look up to. She credited the man for believing in her and telling her that her fiery tongue and intrepid spirit were attributes to be celebrated, while she was told for a large chunk of her life that they were habits to be purged.

"Maybe you should walk down to the morgue and look up your last big break." He pointed to the door on his left. The door led down to the archives room, and it was full of stories that were yesterday's news, including a story she wanted to stay buried for good. "I know you haven't forgotten what happened. By the way you write stories about Wisneski and Holt, I know you haven't learned yet."

"But this guy is pure evil, Gabe. I can feel it."

Gabriel relaxed and stood up straight, exhaling to gather his thoughts. "This newspaper is changing, kid. Locklear is breathing down my neck, and pretty soon, this paper will be a den of puff pieces and crony journalism—"

"So let's get one last good story before all of our front pages are new bakeries and Little Heaven's oldest relative." Simone raised both arms, giving Gabriel the misty-eyed puppy dog pout that she rightly knew he could not say no to. Gabriel sighed again, shaking his head.

"God, you remind me of me sometimes. I don't want to see any mudslinging in your articles. Truth is a just enough cause. You keep your head down, and you keep your mouth closed as much as you physically can. Be slow to speak, and maybe others will be slow to anger."

Simone smiled and hugged Gabriel around his neck. He smiled and patted her shoulder. She let go of him and briskly walked out of his office. "You will not regret this, Gabe. Who knows? This may be the big break that will finally convince Locklear to write real stories and maybe even give me your office."

"You'll have to kill me first, Jaws," Gabriel yelled, laughing as he spoke.

"Don't tempt me, old-timer," Simone shot back.

As she pulled up to the abandoned house, Simone unbuckled her seatbelt and reached into the backseat to get her bag, checking to make sure everything she needed was there. Phone, backup iPad, two pens, a notepad with Spongebob Squarepants on the cover, and a pack of gummy bears. The tools of her trade. Seeking out the truth no matter how ugly it was.

She exited her car, surprised to see that she was the first to arrive at the crime scene even after stopping by and chatting a bit with her coworker Jackson. Was this story her destiny? Was it ordained by someone bigger than her? Simone was not sure, but what she did know was that she could feel how big this story was going to be. This was more significant than putting Ezra Wisneski and Clarke Holt's feet to the coals. This was even more astronomical than the Winter Narcotics scandal five years ago. She reminded herself, ever since that story became her famous fifteen minutes of fame, that the power of truth without love can be as brutal as taking a life.

Simone sauntered to the building and waited for the officers on duty to exit the crime scene. She had worked as a reporter long enough to know that barging into a crime scene of any caliber was a sure-fire way to get manhandled back to your car. Waiting around for permission, on the other hand, was what was twice as frustrating. Knowing the truth was so close but red tape and bureaucracy kept her from grasping it set her teeth on edge.

As fifteen excruciating minutes ticked by, Simone impatiently tapped her foot on the cracked sidewalk. It was surrounded by a lawn that was overgrown and riddled with weeds and ant hills, complete eye sores that would be the bane of any homeowners association if anyone would ever dare live in this scab of a neighborhood. The door of the abandoned home gradually creaked open, and Simone's eyebrows raised in alarm when the officer exiting the dilapidated building was none other than Leroy Stone. His eyes were squinted, probably from adjusting to the strangely hot November sun. As his face relaxed, his eyes widened when they glimpsed the audience standing outside ready to meet him. The press. And much worse, Simone "Jaws" Garcia.

"Detective Stone," Simone called in her most professional voice. She and Stone had a history, encounters and exchanges they both wished would remain just that: history. "Would you like to offer a quote for *The Trumpet*? My readers want to know what you think this killer's plan is."

Leroy stood as still as a statue. He was not sure whether he should go back into the house of horrors or face a reaper from his past in the appearance of this young woman. He decided to take another route, grunting and shaking his head while walking past her like the apparition she is. Immediately following him was Commissioner Stricker, who was just as displeased to see who showed up. She stopped and looked down at the small Hispanic reporter with a face full of disdain and familiarity.

"What do you think you're doing here, Garcia?" Marleen demanded, crossing her arms around her stomach.

"Truth is a just enough cause, Marleen. And you know I'm always looking for a couple of just causes," Simone retorted with a smile, lifting up her phone to Marleen's mouth and pressing the record button on the screen. "Care to indulge me?"

Marleen feigned a chuckle in return and firmly pressed the pause button. "Off the record, he still hasn't forgiven you for what happened with Jacob. I have, but I don't forget so easily. And that's *Commissioner* to you, missy."

Simone lowered her hand and sighed. "Look, you want to find this guy. I need another big break. I already promised my boss that there would be no mudslinging in this story even if the killer is a maniacal, psychopathic monster."

Marleen scoffed. "We both know your promise is a sham. When do you ever stay true to a word unless it's one being used to degrade a victim in another article?"

Simone winced at her opposer's statement. She steadied her breath, reminding herself how desperately she wanted this story. "But I am willing to promise you, whatever you need me to do, I want to help you solve this case. I will go back to my old, mudslinging ways, however, if you don't cooperate."

Marleen's eyebrows raised in shock at the young woman's tenacity. She saw a bit of herself in Simone, a fire she couldn't deny. Chuckling under her breath, Marleen turned around to walk back into the crime scene but then stopped to take a look back at the reporter. "Come on, Jaws."

Simone hurriedly followed Marleen into the dimly lit room. The first thing she noticed were the words on the wall. They shaped the empty area where the corpse had been. Stepping forward for a closer look, Simone brushed passed the medical examiner, who was zipping up Ezra Wisneski into a body bag. Her head tilted with curiosity. These sentences seemed familiar, from a time when she was a young Catholic girl going to mass with her mother. Though the memory was burned into the back of her mind, she shook it away with determination. Focusing on the current task was more important than traveling down an undesirable path, so she whipped out her phone to take pictures as Marleen spoke.

"Yesterday, Tuesday night, Ezra Wisneski never made it home. He went out to pick up something at his campaign office and disappeared.

At around noon, a package was delivered. The office manager did not see a truck or anyone drop it off. It just appeared there. Upon opening it, a human tongue was found in some ice with a return address printed on one of the box's flaps. The cops followed up on the address and discovered Mr. Wisneski taped to the wall, mouth sewn shut, with a creepy poem or something bordering the body—"

"Bible verse," a voice said, interrupting Marleen's flow of information.

Startled at the interjection, Marleen and Simone looked up to see Leroy standing in the doorway, leaning against the post and staring at the words on the wall.

"What?" Marleen cocked her head in confusion.

"It's a Bible verse. Exodus 22. It's also a part of the Talmud. One of the 613

commandments that the Jews had to follow."

"You're right!" Simone suddenly exclaimed. "I remember studying this as a little girl when I was in Catholic school."

"You're a believer, huh?"

"Oh, not-not anymore. Bad experiences with religion."

"You and me, both, kiddo," Marleen said, looking again at the wall. "Never saw anything I needed in a church. No offense, by the way, Stone."

"None taken," Leroy said with a shrug. "Wisneski is a Jewish name, right?" He continued, walking toward the wall.

"I think so. Why, do you think his race had anything to do with this?" Marleen asked.

"No, no. I just find it odd that he killed a man of Jewish descent using a scripture verse from the Talmud to tell us why he did it."

"Maybe he's just telling us..." Simone paused to chew on her pen. "Ezra Wisneski was a cold, calculated, and greedy slumlord that—"

"It's disrespectful to speak badly about the dead, sweetheart," Leroy interrupted.

Simone rolled her eyes and snapped her head toward Leroy. "But it's the truth. Would you rather me not speak at all, Detective?"

"I'd prefer it."

"And I'd prefer it if you two shut up and focus." Marleen interjected, her voice echoing through the empty house. "Simone, please, continue."

"As I was saying," Simone tried again, glaring at Leroy as he stared her down, "that evicted one-hundred families out of his crummy, backwater apartments because they couldn't afford both rent and food on the table. That's at least two or three hundred people out on the street or in homeless shelters. No home, no food, and no way to keep themselves warm."

"Sounds to me like you agree with this guy," Leroy grumbled under his breath.

"What I am trying to say is that Wisneski could have extended their rent, but he chose to stay silent and let people suffer."

Leroy stood up straight to meet Marleen's eyes and silently beg her for some help. Instead, she pointed at Simone with her head as if signifying how on a roll the young reporter was. Leroy grunted disapprovingly and turned to Simone to add in his two cents.

"By that logic, you're saying this guy is some kind of antihero."

"In a way, yes. But does this look like the work of a hero to you?" Simone pondered aloud.

All three glanced down at the body bag being carted out and then at the wall covered in dark red paint. Leroy finally answered after a few beats of silence. "If that's true and we're taking what he said seriously, he is going to kill again."

"Exactly," Simone said. Her voice was low and serious. "It's just a matter of when."

OUXLT

III

DOCTORS AND GRAVE DIGGERS

"No. No. No, no, no, no, no, *no*. Absolutely *not*. Not in a million years. No. No." Leroy jumped out of his chair in Marleen's office and paced around the clean and organized workspace. A week of searching for The Seamstress turned up unsuccessful. None of the team's tactics were working. There was nothing else they could contribute to the LHPD in finding this guy, and the commissioner was proposing a fresh mind and pair of eyes to assist Leroy in the case. She patiently waited for her friend to sit back down, not raising her voice or even speaking at all. She had known him long enough to realize that he would react this way. It was all about how certain ideas were presented to Leroy.

"C'mon, you know that this is a good idea."

"*No.* I do not do partners. Ever. I don't even wanna be your partner."

"You haven't had a partner in five years, Daniel. Who's gonna watch your back?"

"Nobody. That's exactly the way I like it. I don't need nobody, and I've never needed nobody."

Marleen bit her lip to stop the words that she eagerly wanted to say from flying out like a plague of locusts. Leroy noticed her restraint, rubbing the top of his bald head while pacing around.

"What? You have something to say. Go on and say it."

Marleen sighed then spoke with her eyes closed. "It's that kinda attitude that made Jaqueline leave."

15

Leroy's mouth hit the floor. He was always amazed by the sheer amount of honesty the woman could dole out. It was harsh, but it was never cruel. Marleen Stricker knew exactly what needed to be said at all times. His only friend. The only person he could open up to. Leroy slumped into his chair with his head in his hands, breathing deeply to compose himself. His mind ran through how his marriage crumbled after Jacob died and how he felt responsible. He could audibly hear Jaqueline's voice demanding that he needed to open up to her and impotently watched her leave because he couldn't live up to her expectations. He stared at Marleen with a look of discomfort but with a hint of contentedness.

"Man," Leroy said with an embarrassed chuckle. "You really know how to make an old man feel bad, Marleen."

"Look, if you're old, then I am, too. And I am not about to admit that to anyone, least of all you."

Their laughter filled the room. For a moment, it felt like they were back at Big Joe's Donut Shop drinking coffee and laughing at the stupid jokes and stories Jacob would tell them. He would sit on one side of the booth, and Leroy and Marleen would sit together on the other. Long before he met Jaqueline, and long before the Winter Narcotics scandal put this sleepy town on the map. Leroy hadn't been to Big Joe's in five years. He was not even sure that it was open anymore.

"Look, Daniel. I know you don't need help." Marleen finally said as the laughter died down. "I agree with you one hundred percent. But you can't act like y'all didn't work like clockwork together at the Wisneski crime scene. She's got a good head on her shoulders."

Leroy pursed his lips and shrugged. "You're the boss, Commissioner. You're the one that signs my paychecks every two weeks."

Marleen smiled and shook her head. "For years, I thought it was going to be you behind this desk, signing the checks, calling the shots."

"Well, we all thought a lot of things, but here we are," Leroy said, looking out the office window.

"You were always the best cop between the three of us even after you took your vow of silence. Always doing paperwork as quickly as it hit your desk, tackling ours sometimes when we were behind. Making sure we all wore our vests in *any* situation," Marleen said.

"Nah, Jacob was the brains. I was always the muscle. You had both *and* kept us in line. It worked for a long time. Until it didn't."

"I don't know if you noticed, but that little woman is going to need some muscle in her court if she is going to take on The Seamstress. She's just lucky you've got a good head on your shoulders, too."

Leroy's insightful visage creeped into a goofy grin. "You break me down, and you build me back up. How exactly do you want me to feel?"

"I want you to feel like what you're doing matters, Daniel. I know you're not one who's keen on sharing with people, but even someone like you needs to know what he's doing is right."

Leroy nodded in agreement. He opened his mouth only to close it again, struggling to find the words to convey his thoughts. Finally, he said, "Ever since Jacob died, I feel like I have just stopped caring about it all. My wife, you, the greater good, Little Heaven. I could feel myself sinking further into my own self-isolation. It's like—"

"Like you're digging your own grave?" Marleen finished. "Yeah, I feel that way, too. We both went through a lot when Jacob died, but I realized that what I say and do matters. I am not ready to just give up and die. I think Jacob would want you to press on in the same manner."

Leroy nodded his head again and grunted in agreement. Marleen sighed and leaned back in her chair, chuckling to herself.

"Ya know, Jacob always said we would end up together, you and me. I don't think he meant working together again," Marleen smiled softly. Leroy's eyes raised. They exchanged a moment, and then, he stuttered, trying to find the right thing to say in this sudden sea of awkward silence. Before anything substantial came out of Leroy's mouth, Sharon, Marleen's secretary, rapped on the door and immediately walked in without invitation.

"Excuse me, Commissioner," Sharon said hurriedly, "a package just arrived at Holt Oil Company. It's The Seamstress again."

Marleen and Leroy sprang into action, grabbing their things and running through the plexiglass office door.

"You're joking. Seriously. Tell me you're joking, Gabe." Simone and Gabriel sat in his colorful vintage office. It felt more like a man cave or a game room than an office, Simone thought. All of the toys and posters and valuables would make someone like her lose her focus. Her mind jumped from reading the fine print of Gabriel's movie posters to racing over the handful of scathing bylines that she was more than ready to paint on the front of *The Trumpet*.

She thought she was getting another routine slap on the wrist for writing about local pastor Wilford Hayfield's constant picketing of Planned Parenthood clinics and funerals of soldiers who died in the line of duty. His story got pushed back from the front page to page four instead because of the Wisneski murder. The feeling of surprise felt almost alien to Simone. Here it was, however, in full force, and it was showing all over her face.

"I am not joking," Gabriel said, beaming with pride for Simone. "I got off the phone with the commissioner last night."

"There's no way he would agree to work with me."

"Ah, don't worry about that. Marleen said she would convince him. Do I need to convince you to work with him?"

"More like you need to convince me you're not playing me for a sucker."

"I want you to know that it's not going to be easy. He is a hard nut to crack. And it's only been a few short years since the Winter scandal."

"Yeah," Simone replied sheepishly. "He wasn't too happy to see me last Tuesday. I hope he knows how terrible I feel about what happened because of my article."

"Maybe you'll get a chance to tell him yourself," Gabriel offered. He leaned forward in his chair, which was Simone's clue to listen carefully to what he is about to say. "I'm counting on you to be the face of this paper. Do not turn this case into a personal vendetta like you did the Winter scandal. Repeat after me. 'I am not Wonder Woman.'"

Simone groaned but repeated nonetheless. "I am not Wonder Woman."

"Good. I am going to lunch, so I will see you later. I'll send a text if I hear any updates on the case."

Simone jumped up excitedly, rearing to get back to work.

"And, Jaws?"

Simone stopped at the doorway and looked back. "Yeah, boss?"

"Don't think you're off the hook for that Hayfield profile. Now that Caesar's Ghost Publishing has taken over *The Trumpet*, Locklear is royally pissed at you. You're gonna meet with him on the 12th." He paused a proud smile creeping across his face, one that he was trying to hide. "Good job, kid. Seek that truth no matter what it takes."

"Thanks, Gabe! Have a good lunch."

Simone turned out the door and bumped into Jackson Taylor, the advertisement representative for *The Trumpet*. He was short and skinny with black stringy hair that he usually had slicked back, but today, it was in front of his eyes. The black hoodie he wore was part of his usual attire even though business casual was the norm at *The Trumpet*. He always kept to himself, and he had never really made any friends despite working for the paper for almost a year now. Every time he saw Simone, though, he lit up, and an animated personality hidden behind his outward sheepish nature would shine through. Today was not one of those times.

"Oh, my God, I am so sorry, Jack!" She was the only one who called him Jack. It usually made him smile, but today it had no effect on him.

"It's alright, Jaws," he said, avoiding eye contact. He dusted his worn black hoodie off as if she had left residue on him from running into his torso head first. "I read your profile about Hayfield. No one gets any slack from you, huh?"

Simone smiled sarcastically. Jack was also the only one brave enough to debate with her even though he was nowhere near as good as she was at countering points. "Does a hate-filled goblin like him deserve slack?"

"I mean, I dunno. What if he's getting all of this 'turn or burn' crap from God? He says he's a prophet."

"If he is a prophet of God, then I am a medical doctor. Would you like your brain surgery at 9am or 10?"

"Look, I don't like the guy either. But everyone deserves a fair shake, don't they?"

"Not if they treat my city like it's going to hell in a hand basket," Simone said triumphantly.

"Even though it kind of is right now. Ya know. With the whole Seamstress thing."

Jackson always had a dark streak when it came to his humor, but Simone laughed with him more often than not. On this particular occasion, the laugh was more nervous than hearty. "Anyway, I was just heading out."

"Oh, are you going to lunch? Can I come?"

Jackson's eyes darted from left to right "Uh, n-no. I was actually just leaving. I'm gonna take some personal days. Things are getting, uh, kinda crazy around here. Especially with Caesar's Ghost taking over."

Before she could say anything more, Jackson turned and briskly walked the opposite away. "I'll see you on the other side, Simone. Adios, amigo."

Simone shook her head at the horrendous pronunciation of two Spanish words that any 4-year-old could learn off of a rerun of *Dora the Explorer*. She simply told him goodbye before bee-lining to her office. As soon as she sat down, her phone began vibrating. It was a message from Gabriel.

> *Just got a call from the commissioner. They found another human tongue. I'll let you find out who it is. 5675 Orchard Leaf Avenue. Find the truth, Jaws. - G*

In one fell swoop, Simone grabbed her bag, flipped off her office light, and was out the door on her way to what she believed was the most important story of her life.

RB

IV

EVERY JOINT AND MOTIVE

The battered corpse of Oil Executive Clark Holt clung to the wall of the abandoned gas station with the same look of terror and repentance that Wisneski wore, the last face he would ever make.

Leroy and Simone traipsed around the crime scene, soaking in every detail. The station they stood in lay abandoned for 10 years. It used to be called Gas-N-Go. It was a mom-and-pop corner store where you could still get homemade taffy, and it even had a cafe where you could get some of the best fried chicken for at least fifty miles. An elderly couple by the names of Jonathan and Marjorie Hicks ran the place, and it always felt like home. Leroy remembered trying their spicy ribs and watching Marleen and Jacob tear up in pain over the heat, and Simone remembered this was the only place she could buy Cheerwine in the whole city. It was her dad's favorite, and she would always go back and buy two in his memory.

However, HoltCo rolled in fifteen years ago, and allegedly, the story is that Clarke Holt himself paid the Hicks a visit, offering to buy their pride and joy for a substantial amount of money. Jonathan refused because his plan was to leave Gas-N-Go to his son. Holt was not a man who took no for an answer, and the week after Jonathan stood his ground, Little Heaven's favorite truck stop was ransacked. In the kitchen were scattered pots and pans among destroyed appliances. What was left of the merchandise wouldn't have amounted to ten dollars, and of course, the money in the safe was gone without a trace.

Leroy was the detective assigned to that case, and he remembered Holt paying the Hicks another visit to lament the tragedy that befell this establishment. He offered the money again, and they refused a second time. Three more robberies occurred on that location, and the Hicks were forced to close up shop. Instead of paving over the establishment and putting up one of HoltCo's soulless corporate gas stations, Holt left it standing as a testament to the power he wielded over the businesses in Little Heaven. Ever since then, if Holt wanted a local business gone, all he had to do was show up and ask nicely for the owners to pack their bags, shut their mouths, and take the money. Leroy tried for years to connect HoltCo to what happened with Gas-N-Go, but there was no evidence other than the coincidence that Holt showed up after the first robbery.

But what did all of that smooth-talking and big money get him in the end? A target on his back and someone brave enough to exact their own demented form of justice. A swift end to a life of greed and corruption. Simone and Leroy stared at the husk of a man who destroyed the livelihoods of many citizens of Little Heaven for years.

"Good riddance," Simone concluded, squinting with righteous indignation at the mangled corpse.

Leroy shifted his gaze toward Simone, visually disgusted at the short phrase that had escaped her mouth. "Now is not the time, kid."

Simone ignored the grizzled detective's comment and commenced sweeping the area, careful not to disturb any part of the crime scene. She read aloud the inscription that perfectly traced Clarke Holt's body. This message still had that flowy language and religious overtones as the last, but in contrast, it read more like an Instagram comment from a lifestyle influencer.

"Speak what is good, or remain silent," Simone read aloud. "That doesn't sound like any Bible verse I've heard before." She waited for Leroy to chime in, but he remained quiet. With a tinge of frustration in the back of her throat, Simone spoke again, this time to the walls "Considering the sheer amount of all the people Holt burned, it would seem that the suspect list is probably in the hundreds."

Simone waited another moment for Leroy to respond. He still continued to survey the crime scene without even looking at her. She grew impatient and began to speak with extra volume. "I just think that whoever did this is *someone connected to both men!*" Her words were punctuated and rhythmic, aimed at earning Leroy's attention. He finally caved to her prodding, still without looking at her.

"Yep, this phrase is definitely not from the Bible."

"Are you even listening to me?"

"Do you not see that I am working?" Leroy shot back.

Answering a question with a question. The easiest way to get on Simone Garcia's bad side. "Okay, you obviously have a problem. Let's go ahead and hash it out now."

The CSI workers froze for a moment, looking between the two of them. They longed to tell her about the legendary Stone Mode, the story where the detective surveys every part of the crime scene before ever saying a word. Without an uttered word, Leroy served the whole group a fiery glare that turned them back to their work.

Leroy finally circled back around to Simone, his six-foot one frame towering over her five-foot three physique. He peeked down at her, and the slight head turn felt more judgmental than maybe even Leroy himself intended. His voice was a gruff whisper, and his eyes were filled with irritation. "This is neither the time or the place to hash out personal matters. The choice to work with you was made *for* me, not *by* me. I don't have to like working with you. So when we are at a crime scene together, stop talking and *be professional.*"

Simone rolled her eyes at Leroy's snappy instructions as he turned and walked back to his work. She looked around at the brutal act of violence that had occurred here, a sickening fossil in the city's history and its citizens' memory. Was this story worth working with this strong, mysterious cliché of a man? Part of her was not sure, but the rest of her still yearned for the truth. Who was this person? Why kill these men? What was he trying to tell the citizens of Little Heaven? What was he trying to tell her?

"Come on," Leroy said, jolting Simone from her thoughts. "Let's head back to the precinct. We apparently have a lot to discuss." He then turned on his heel, leaving the remains of what could be Gas-N-Go with Simone following behind him.

"So you're telling me that, so far, you have no idea who the killer could be?" Marleen sat back in her chair, massaging her temples. She, Leroy, and Simone had been workshopping this case for hours with no end in sight. Their white-and-cork-board combination was overflowing with pictures, newspaper articles, yarn, and tacks, everything they could muster to track down the murderer of Holt and Wisneski. Powerful and corrupt men killed for their sins. Killed the same way with their tongues ripped out and mouths sewn shut. Phrases written on the walls they were nailed to. One was clearly a Bible verse, specifically a passage from the Talmud. The other was nowhere in the Bible at all. After a quick Google search, Simone found that it was a verse from the Quran, which only offered up more questions than answers.

"Look, we have a motive," Simone said through a long yawn. "We just have missing pieces. What baffles me the most is that Quran passage. It doesn't make a lot of sense."

"Do we know if Holt was a Muslim?' Marleen asked, looking over at Leroy. He hadn't said anything for the duration of the session. He merely sat back and let the women take the lead.

"No, he never claimed to be," Simone responded instead.

"It could be the fact that HoltCo was an oil company," Leroy chimed.

Simone and Marleen shared a look of surprise. Leroy was already a man of few words. When he *did* speak, it was like reading a book for which you would expect to take a test the next day. The listener did his or her utmost to hang on to every word.

"Explain," Marleen prompted.

"A good chunk of our oil comes from the Middle East, doesn't it?"

"I thought most of our oil came from Canada," Simone nervously countered, hoping to contribute some insight.

"Well, now, the country of Canada doesn't have a specific holy book, does it?"

"That still doesn't make any sense. Why go from Judaism to Islam in just two kills?"

"That part seems obvious," Leroy replied matter-of-factly. "He doesn't want to give himself away."

Simone scrunched her face. *Was it* that obvious? Was it merely a red herring so they would lose the trail of breadcrumbs The Seamstress left behind?

"Maybe we should play both videos and see if we hear or notice anything important we may have missed before." Simone said in a huff.

Simone nodded and played the first video of the killer and Wisneski off YouTube. After it ended, she began to rewind randomly, starting and stopping at different sections of the clip to see if some clue, some string begging to be pulled would rear its ugly head so the three of them could unravel this mystery and find out why it all ensued. Or even more pressing for time's sake, who was the killer targeting next? Simone then heard The Seamstress utter the demonic phrase "baptize every devil in Little Heaven with oil and set their corpses aflame."

"Do you notice anything specific when he says this line?"

Marleen and Leroy leaned forward, scanning every inch of the frame for anything unordinary. She played it again two more times. When the word "oil" was uttered, The Seamstress emphasized it with fist pound to the table.

"Oh, my God," Marleen murmured. "He told us who he was targeting next. How did we miss that?"

Leroy sat grim as a tomb. Simone turned the laptop around to face her again so she could pull up the second video. "It's not as much about what comes out of the victims' mouths. It's more about what they *don't* say and what they do."

Simone clicked the play button as she spun the laptop around once more. It opened up the same as before: a dimly lit room with one lightbulb, a table, and a chair. The Seamstress was sitting down looking deeply into the eyes of anyone who would dare watch such a mini horror film. His monologue was different this time, albeit just as malevolent as the first.

"Hello, again, Little Heaven. I hope you are well. I hope that those who hail me as a hero and, more importantly, those who seek to spin my actions as villainy are listening carefully."

All three spectators in the office jumped back in their seats as The Seamstress slammed his hands on the table, exclaiming, *"Awake, awake, oh, sleeper! And rise from the dead!"*

He then calmly leaned back and panned the camera over v Clarke Holt, who was beaten and tied to a chair. The oil guru's eyes were full of rage at the inconvenience of being kidnapped by a lunatic.

"What? Do you think this scares me? I've hired goons scarier than you! You want me to be afraid of you, ya piece of trash?! Well, that ain't—"

Holt's condemnation ceased when The Seamstress entered the frame. His eyes darted to the left as the killer flipped open a butterfly knife, suddenly brimming with unbridled terror.

"Wait, please. You don't have to do this. Please, *no!*"

The scream that crawled out of Holt's throat was worse than when Wisneski died. Maybe it was the fact that Holt's final moments were actually pictured on camera and that not even someone as intimidating as he was refrained from showing fear against this monster from the depths of hell. Just like before, the killer's garbled voiceover stung the ears of the listeners.

"What else is there to say about Clarke Holt? Greed. Selfishness. Pride. He waltzed around Little Heaven, *your city*, as a king taking what he pleased and terrifying those who got in his way. He used his voice, a voice that God only gives to some, not as a tool to enhance the greater good but as a weapon to raze livelihoods and tear down dreams."

Suddenly, the footage flipped back to a close up of The Seamstress's mask. "I made you a promise in my first proclamation. The city of Little Heaven will be purged of the impurities who wield their unclean lips as a weapon. They may hide behind a veil of righteousness, but they are wolves in sheep's clothing. I have spoken, and now I shall do."

Just like that, The Seamstress vanished those red and blue buttons sending chills down Leroy's spine. He slid down in his chair, devastated at the magnitude of this case. "How on Earth did we get here?"

"It's hard to tell. But we have to keep going. We will stop this guy," Marleen promised, placing her hand on Leroy's. He looked up at her, feeling the color leave his skin but also feeling reassured that Marleen Stricker was here to back him up. "We all will."

Leroy smiled at Marleen. It was a grin that even Simone could not ignore. This man was hurt by a world that does not care that you are the good guy. It only cares about taking what you love and throwing it in the trash. His delighted expression then turned into an epiphany that caused him to jump out of his chair. "Awake, O sleeper!" Leroy exclaimed. "Do you know what that is?"

"No, but it certainly sounds biblical in nature," Simone suggested, listening intently.

"Well, yes, of course. But he did that for a reason. That's our clue, and better yet, it's a cry of protest. Do you know who screamed this at me when I told them to disperse Mrs. Lowe's son's funeral?"

"No, way," Marleen said, jerking herself up from the table. "The Eden's Branch people?"

"*Yes!*" Leroy yelled excitedly. He quickly grabbed Simone's laptop and typed feverishly. Simone had never seen this level of energy from the detective. She stood with the two accomplished investigators piecing the components of the murderer's threat together bit by bit.

"So The Seamstress's next target is—"

"Wilford Hayfield," Leroy finished, revealing the laptop screen, which bore the man's character profile. "We need to get to Eden's Branch Baptist Church. Stat."

ARBRWP

27

V

SEAT OF SCOFFERS

"Detective, Ms. Garcia. Reverend Hayfield will see you now. Right this way, please."

A tall, skinny woman who wore far too much makeup and used far too much hairspray led the detective and the reporter down the sepia cave of a hallway meant to be the main offices of Eden's Branch Baptist Church. Leroy and Simone uncomfortably looked around at the walls decorated with stained glass windows and wooden crosses. Eyes full of discrimination and judgement peered over computer monitors and mounds of paperwork.

Neither Leroy nor Simone was comfortable in a place like this, albeit raised in religious backgrounds. This church felt more like a doctor's office than a place of worship, but then again, hospitals, like churches, are supposed to be full of people who know they are sick and desperately want to get better. On this occasion, all the clergymen and women were merely people who pretended to be healthy and pushed all the sick people out with their God-hates-you attitude and ice-cold shoulders. Not one of them spoke to the detective or the reporter, and it seemed like the only nice person among them was the secretary leading them through this lion's den.

The lady turned a corner and straight into a large office full of photos, books about theology and the end times, and a large stained glass cross behind a desk. She motioned for Leroy and Simone to sit, and they followed suit. Though she left the room, her greeting could still be heard by the visitors.

"Well, hey, there, Reverend. There's some colored cop and his Mexican reporter friend here to see you."

Simone whirled around at the ever-present echo of racism. "My family is from Ecuador, you clown-faced—"

"Stop," Leroy quickly whispered, placing a hand on Simone's shoulder. "We are in enemy territory now, so just follow my lead and play it cool. Please?"

The softness in Leroy's voice surprised her. She realized that he, too, was an outsider. They were two refugees in a building where they were not wanted, and even though he chastised her, his statement made her feel like he had her back. She nodded and spun back around, waiting patiently as Wilford Hayfield waddled into the room.

He was a petite man, one of the oldest people alive in Little Heaven. His age was evident from a visible hunch and comb over to hide the male pattern baldness. Other than the white and royal blue orthopedic shoes for his arthritis and a bolo tie around his neck with an inscription of an olive branch, he wore the usual preacher attire. Simone chuckled at the irony of someone who purported peace but was known for causing dissent and unrest in the city.

Evidence of this lifestyle emanated from the photos of Hayfield and company on the wall. Simone noted that he had shaken hands with every reprobate that lived within the city limits. He was there when HoltCo was first opened, exchanging pleasantries with Clarke Holt, and he was there showing his support for Ezra Wisneski, probably because he bailed his cult members out of jail a few times. He was even shaking Micheal Locklear's hand when Caesar's Ghost slid their way into buying *The Trumpet*. They were all here in these captured memories, all the people Simone despised and wanted to see brought to justice more than anything. She shook her head, realizing that, somehow, greed and selfishness were more powerful than hate.

Wilford made his way to his chair, and Leroy stood up, extending a hand for him to take. "Reverend Hayfield."

Hayfield waved his hand at the gesture like he was swatting at a fly. He finally sat and sternly looked them both in the eyes. Simone was unsure if his face sagged into this rigid scowl because of his wrinkles and deteriorating elasticity or if it was the immense amount of demonic hatred for her and Leroy that made his face contort in such a way.

"What do you two want?" Hayfield barked. The words stung more than Hayfield knew, but then again, maybe he did.

Leroy dove in without skipping a beat. "Forgive us for intruding on your busy day, Reverend, but we are here because we believe that The Seamstress is going to make an attempt on your life."

Hayfield erupted into a wheezy cackle, one so hoarse it sounded like he would drop dead from lack of oxygen. "Nonsense, I will be just fine. Thank you, you may leave now."

"At least let us show you the proof," Simone pleaded. Hayfield shot an evil eye over to the young reporter.

"Do you think I'm daft? That I don't watch the news, young lady? Ever since you tried to sink your teeth into me with that pack of lies that you called an article, I've been sure to catch late-night broadcasts. As if I don't deal with your company enough after that nincompoop Taylor boy complained about me not buying an ad from him."

Simone closed her eyes and counted down from ten, stifling the urge to verbally rip this man's head off. "I was simply writing the truth. It's my job."

"You made it seem like my protests and civil disobedience were wrong," Hayfield replied. "I am doing the Lord our God's work."

"Oh, yeah? How is screaming at pregnant women and interrupting soldiers' funeral services 'the Lord's work'?" Simone's voice rose. "Sounds like the work of the other guy to me."

Wilford shoved away from his chair in a huff. "Well, I beg your pardon, you dirty—"

"Okay, stop," Leroy yelled, jumping up and extending his hands between Hayfield and Simone. "Mr. Hayfield, please. We are not here to debate with you. We have reason to believe The Seamstress is targeting you, and we would like to offer a protective detail. This is a serious matter, and I do not want anymore...innocent blood spilled in the process."

31

Hayfield pondered the detective's words as he sat back down. "Thank you for that," he said with a smug grin. "But as I said before, I do not need protection from *you* people. The God of angel armies will protect me, and I will not abide the LHPD, an institution that hires corrupt men from the wrong side of the tracks and willingly works with lying immigrant Jezebels who spout libelous accusations at my ministry!" Blood vessels in Hayfield's forehead could be seen from space. "For as it says in first Samuel, 'Do not consider his appearance or his height, for I have rejected him.'" When he was done with his lecture, he relaxed in his chair and you could hear a pin drop in the office.

Simone wanted to jump over the desk and beat this racist fool senseless like she did older boys when she was in middle school. She got up out of her seat, but a strong hand held her shoulder back. Leroy's hand. He already had one foot out the door, and his eyes were dark.

"You people, huh?" His voice was subdued, and his fists were balled up so tight Simone was worried he would pull a muscle. "I think you need to finish reading that verse. 'Do not consider his appearance or his height, for I have rejected him. *The Lord* does not look at the things people look at. People look at outward appearance, but the Lord looks at *the heart*!' And if I were to guess, *Mister* Hayfield, your heart is a sickly, diseased tar pit of an organ that would not know the voice of God if it whispered into your ear with a megaphone!"

Hayfield rose to meet Leroy's gaze, crossing his arms around his chest in absolute offense. "Just who do you think you are?"

Leroy slapped a hand on the preacher's desk, the intense contact reverberating like thunder as if God himself had graced the corner office of Eden's Branch Baptist Church. "I was not done, sir. You have done nothing but cause this community trouble. Picketing weddings you don't agree with, chasing black families out of their homes, but what really gets me is you think you're right. You think your ministry is being blessed by God. Well, I'm not smart enough to discuss such matters, but there is someone in this town who thinks you and your whole operation are going to hell in a hand basket. That person is The Seamstress. He wants you dead, and we haven't figured out how to stop him yet. But you're too proud to take our help. Do you really want that poor secretary out there to find your severed tongue and cry all her makeup off? Now, I'm not giving you a choice on a protective detail." Leroy motioned for his partner as he hustled toward the door without a glimpse back. "Let's go somewhere we are wanted, Simone."

"I'm telling you I don't want your protection!" Hayfield screamed with resentment. He continued, pointing out the door, "Get out of my church! You and your whore have darkened my doorstep long enough! And if I so much as smell an LHPD patrol car outside my home or my church, I will sue you and your department for everything you've got."

Leroy gladly stormed out of the hell-hole, his feet hitting the black pavement so hard he almost barreled to the ground. When he was far enough away from those claustrophobic walls and fundamentalist asphyxiation, he paused to catch his breath. Simone bolted up to him and waited for him to finish reclaiming freedom. Once he had regained composure, Leroy looked over at the small woman, and they both laughed. They laughed like there had been an inside joke they were holding the whole time, like Hayfield had had something on his face or his shirt that they couldn't wait to lampoon. It was something in their souls, however, that made them laugh this way, not because their experience was funny but because it was tragically sad.

"Never seen you get so fired up, Stone," Simone said.

"Yeah, well, I never liked him. Plus, he insulted you, and I was not gonna allow that. You got a couple of right hooks in there as well."

"What can I say? It's who I am," Simone beamed.

"Come on. Let's get back to Marleen. Hayfield doesn't want our help, but maybe we can cut The Seamstress off before he kills again."

As they reached the car, Simone's phone rang. "You go ahead. It's probably someone from *The Trumpet*." She looked at her screen, but there wasn't a single digit. Only a word. *Unknown*. The word covered the picture of her father on her lock screen. Simone pulled back her long curly hair and pressed the answer button. "Hello? Who is this?"

A distorted voice matched her question with a question. "How was it, sitting in the seat of scoffers?" The Seamstress was now directly reaching out.

"About as well as expected. How did you get this number?"

"Don't worry about how I'm speaking to you. Only worry about what. I've been watching you closely, Garcia. Your never-ending crusade for the truth is...inspirational." The Seamstress laughed in a manner that made Simone pull the phone away from her ear.

"Glad that you read *The Trumpet*," Simone sarcastically retorted, trying to hide the fear creeping up her spine. "What do you want from me?"

"What I want is for you to find me. I want you to figure out this Minotaur's Labyrinth of a puzzle."

"Then make it easy for us. Turn yourself in."

The Seamstress howled in amusement. "Now, we cannot make it too easy for old Detective Stone, can we? I only want you to find me because, if you do, maybe you'll realize that you and I are the same."

"I am nothing like you. I seek the truth. You just kill people who are wrong."

"That's the only rule I want you to drop. I seek the truth, too. My way just requires more...bloodshed. Love without truth is hypocrisy after all."

"And truth without love is brutality."

"Something you know very well, Jaws." His use of her nickname shook Simone to her core. "You know that the truth is powerful enough to drive a man to suicide. I am simply hanging up the noose."

"I know you didn't call me to debate the philosophy behind your killings. Say what you need to say and leave me alone."

The Seamstress was quiet. Simone could not believe that she actually offended a serial killer. She tapped her foot for every second she awaited a reply.

"Fine," The Seamstress caved. "I will take Wilford Hayfield five days from today. I will sever his liar's tongue from his unclean mouth at 2398 Whirling Seed Drive at 3 p.m." Simone knew the location by heart. It was the old abandoned church that Wilford Hayfield ran out of town for having an eighty-five percent African American congregation. "If you keep my secret, I will know you are on my side and only the wolf in sheep's clothing will die. However, if the cops arrive, I will turn my divine wrath against one of them. Maybe it could even be a certain detective."

Simone chewed on the inside of her cheek. How could she keep this phone call to herself? Maybe it was best for everyone if she treaded lightly and went this alone as the killer suggested. Did she really care if Hayfield met his fate? She weighed the heavy decision for a few moments. "The choice is yours," The Seamstress noted as if reading Simone's mind. This proposition was immediately followed by a tritone of beeps signifying the end of the call.

Wrestling with this information so freely given by the hunted killer, Simone's mind began to race.

BCJH

VI

IGNORANCE OR INFIRMITY

It was 8 a.m., and today was the day that Hayfield's mouth would be sewn shut forever. Simone sat speechless, clutching one of Gabriel's Bibles in her lap like the steady foundation he claimed it was. Gabriel was propped against the wall to her left rubbing the bridge of his nose as Micheal Locklear, CEO for Caesar's Ghost Publishing House, sat in Gabe's chair and prattled on and on about how we are to treat our investors. His black leather jacket squeaked with every stomp of his combat boots. He looked more like Danny Zuko if he and Sandy had a nasty divorce and was going through his midlife crisis.

This was not her first meeting, for she had sat in this exact position many times since the publishing house took over. She would probably sit in this position many times after today. Her disregard for Locklear's lecture was caused by her internal conflict to tell Leroy about The Seamstress's sadistic trolley problem: say nothing and Wilford Hayfield dies or tell Marleen and Leroy about The Seamstress's plan and someone else dies *with* him.

An impossible task. While she wanted justice for all of the people that Hayfield had hurt over the years, brutally murdering him was surely off of the table. However, someone from LHPD getting murdered for her choice to tell them did not seem ideal either. She had to come up with something soon, but she had to get out of this meeting with her job intact first.

"Look, Micheal, all I'm saying is that, even though Hayfield supports *The Trumpet*, that doesn't mean that Simone did anything wrong,"

"Mr. Locklear, please," the man scolded, feverishly pulling back his slick black hair with his fingers. Locklear and Gabriel came up together as reporters. They were the Dream Team when they worked on stories. As they got older, Gabriel became more interested in telling real stories, while Locklear only wanted to create bylines that caught the eye and stories that turned pages and made profits. They eventually had a falling out, and Locklear worked his way up the chain to become CEO of a publishing house.

Now, his slimy tentacles were subtly squeezing every ounce of morality out of *The Trumpet*. Gabriel winced, biting his lip as a safety precaution for his job. Many people spoke out against the publishing house taking over, including Gabriel, but whatever bosses to whom he had to adhere told him that he could keep this job if he played along. At this particular moment, Simone wondered if he regretted that arrangement.

"All I'm saying is that, if investors are not happy, then I am not happy," Locklear resolved, now stalking around the office like a lion hunting his prey. "And when I am not happy, I begin to fire people at random. It could be from the bottom, maybe from the mailroom. Maybe that lazy adolescent I keep telling to quit wearing that abominable hoodie in this building. Maybe I'm feeling bold and it could be from the *top*." His eyes rested on Gabriel. Simone knew a threat when she saw one.

"So do you expect me to just lie about these men? To actively ignore the truth in my writings?" Simone squinted her eyes as she locked them with Locklear's.

"Oh, heavens, no, my dear." Locklear slinked up behind her chair and placed both his hands on her shoulders. "I am expecting you to...dance with the truth. Take it for a walk, spin it around, and showcase the parts people want to hear."

Simone stood, shaking out of Locklear's grasp. "How is that any different from lying?"

"Listen to me," Locklear bellowed, wagging his finger at his fiery employee. The raised voice and lack of respect sent Simone back to the days living with her mother after her father died. No one ever understood her drive to tell the truth. Not like Gabriel did. Not like her father. "The people of this city are like children. Treat all of them like you do that degenerate, Jackson. Children should not be told bad news. Bad news is for adults like you and me. Tell the people of Little Heaven bad news much like you would a child. This is what is best for the city. Now that they have this Sewing Killer person running amok."

"It's The Seamstress," Simone corrected. "Do you even read your own paper?

"Whatever. We do not need the negativity, Ms. Garcia. If I did not know any better, I would say that the profiles you wrote about Wisneski, Holt, and Wilford are why they have been targeted in the first place."

Before Simone could rip Locklear a new one, a ring tone disrupted the heat of the moment. She realized her phone was buzzing. It was Leroy, and she knew that she was needed at the precinct. "It's Detective Stone, *sir*. I need to take this."

"Very well. Saved by the bell, I guess. Off you go."

One foot out the door, Simone was stopped by another hand on her shoulder. This time, Locklear's touch felt far too close to her neck.

"Your constant insolence and disregard for authority has been noticed, *Jaws*. I'm not sure if you think this is the hip or cool thing for young people like you to do, but I do not appreciate it. I would be careful what you say from here on out or you may be working for the LHPD permanently. I'm sure you look great in Meter Maid orange and yellow."

Simone grimaced. Locklear had dark, soulless eyes. He was a sad excuse for a man who cared about profit over truth. They exchanged scowls for what felt like an eternity.

"Go ahead, Jaws," Gabriel said, slicing the silence with a knife. "I'll handle this. Just take the Bible with you."

Without another word, Simone left the bright decorated office and answered her phone.

"Hello?"

"Hey, head to the precinct. We may have something."

"Great," Simone replied. "I'll see you soon." She strolled by Jackson's office, only to see a stripped down room and Jackson holding a box of his belongings. Simone stopped in her tracks and leaned in his doorway.

"Jack, what's going on?"

Jackson smiled weakly and shrugged his shoulders. "Locklear finally got tired of me not delivering, I guess." Simone raised her eyebrows in support and a twinge of understanding. Jackson was not the best ad rep *The Trumpet* had, but he did give his best. It was also well-known that Locklear could not stand him.

"It's whatever. It sucks working for him and Gabe anyway, so I'm gonna go out and do something better. Somewhere I'm appreciated."

Simone's face filled with shock. "Jack, I'm—"

Jackson Taylor stormed past her and left the building without saying goodbye. Simone finally understood why he was acting so strangely the other day. Locklear's frustration with the young man's inability to sell ad space for *The Trumpet* had proven inconsolable and he sent the employee packing.

"All I am saying is that there is a connection here and we are just not seeing it."

Leroy paced around the room, his fingers caressing his short, curly beard. It was an inversion of the first brainstorming meeting they had when Simone speculated aloud and he stayed contemplative. Simone twiddled with the laptop, typing in the address of the abandoned church then deleting it while debating with herself about The Seamstress's warning. It was two o'clock in the afternoon. In one hour, Wilford Hayfield would die.

"Are you sure there isn't anything in the video we missed?" Marleen asked with a mouth full of pretzels.

"Yes, we have scanned both videos more times than we can count, and there's nothing new to see. There's gotta be some other connection we don't understand."

Leroy looked to Simone for advice, though she hadn't said a word since she arrived. She cradled her head in her hand, nonchalantly hitting keyboard keys with one finger.

"C'mon, kid, you're killing the room here. You alright?"

Simone snapped to attention. "What? Oh, yeah. I just had a rough meeting with Locklear today."

Leroy dragged a chair over to Simone's, gently entering the seat while patting her on the right shoulder. "Aw, don't let a corporate stiff like him get you down. You're a great reporter, but we gotta stay in the game."

"Don't sweat it, Garcia." Marleen leaned over and playfully punched Simone on the arm. "If I let every bad meeting I've had over the years have its way with me, I'd be retired by now."

They were right. Simone knew she needed to focus, but this problem was far too colossal for her to solve on her own. She was normally the one who used her words to get out of any situation, and she had been spoon-fed necessary information by the very vampire she was determined to pull into the light. However, she felt her hands were tied from using any of it.

Dance with the truth. Take it for a walk, spin it around, and showcase the parts people want to hear. Locklear's words reverberated in her mind like a gong. Simone suddenly gasped, her inner light bulb going off for all to see.

"What is it? Do you have a fresh lead?" Leroy gaped.

Simone eagerly threw herself over the computer, entering a slew of words into the web browser and clicking links at lightning speed. "Do you notice how everything was abandoned when we found each victim's body?"

"Of course, less prying eyes. Efficient working space. Why?" Leroy asked.

"Gas-N-Go. Why was Holt found at Gas-N-Go?"

"Because Holt is a gas tycoon? There are a thousand abandoned gas stations at which The Seamstress could have dropped off Holt."

"Exactly. Think about it. Why did we find him at Gas-N-Go?"

Marleen gasped. "Because Holt ran Gas-N-Go out of business!"

Leroy turned his head. "Well, allegedly. We never had any proof."

"There seemed to be enough for The Seamstress. Think about where we found Wisneski," Simone continued.

"An abandoned house? Because he's a slumlord," Marleen assessed.

"*Exactly*! The Seamstress wanted them to see firsthand what their actions did. An empty, broken down home, a gas station run out of business, and that means to find out where Hayfield is—"

"We need to find a place that would mean something to Hayfield!" Leroy exclaimed. "Holy Spirit Pentecostal! Over on Whirling Seed Drive! Marleen! Call an officer whose route is nearby."

Marleen raised an eyebrow and cleared her throat. "I'm sorry, uh, who is the boss here again?"

Leroy and Simone stopped in their tracks. Marleen laughed heartily, grabbing her walkie-talkie. "I'm just kidding. Calling all units, this is Commissioner Stricker. Anyone nearby Whirling Seed Drive? I need someone to check out the church."

A voice came over the comm. "Yeah, boss. This is Officer Dulvey. We're five minutes away from that location. Standby."

The five minutes that the officer spent getting to the location were excruciating. Simone stared at the clock. It took exactly thirty-seven minutes to get over to that church from the precinct. It was currently 2:42 p.m. The static of the walkie-talkie made Simone jump.

"Commissioner, this is Dulvey. I drove by Whirling Seed Drive. Some guy in a black jacket was walking Old Man Hayfield into the old church. Didn't get an ID on his face, though. Am I clear to investigate?"

"Negative officer, stay back," Marleen hastily answered. "The Seamstress is there. We are on the way with more firepower. Standby for more instructions."

Leroy and Marleen were already mounting up, grabbing their guns and badges, ready to head out the door and end this nightmare forever. Simone stood up to grab her things as well, but Leroy sat her back down with a soft hand on her shoulder. "Hey, hey, where do you think you're going? This is police business. I need you to stay."

"But I have to go! What if something happens?"

"Don't worry, okay?" Leroy said, checking his weapon for bullets. "Marleen's got my back. I'll see you soon, and God willing, we will have this guy in handcuffs when we come back."

As Leroy left the office, Marleen cocked her weapon and winked at Simone, leaving her in the empty office hoping and praying the team would get there in time to save Hayfield and get away before someone died.

Reaching for his hand, Marleen stopped Leroy in the hall.

"Daniel, wait."

He turned around to face his boss. "Yeah?"

She pulled him close, closer than any commissioner and her detective should be, especially at work.

"Jacob always said we would end up together. When this is all over, maybe we—"

Leroy interrupted Marleen with a kiss on her cheek. He placed a hand where he had kissed her and grinned like the Cheshire Cat. "I would love that. More than anything,"

Marleen's face burned bright pink, and she returned the sweet gesture. Setting their gaze on the exit, they clasped each other's hand and ran toward a madman they were determined to unmask.

Simone impatiently waited in the blank meeting room, the walls closing in around her and the clock ticking closer to the deadline. She desperately rummaged through her bag to take her mind off the angst. Her eyes rested on Gabriel's Bible. She decided to flip through its pages. This was a book she hadn't looked at since she was a child. Gabriel's faith in a God who loved him and loved everyone was inspirational, and his dedication to the truth and telling it well was bolstered by his unshakable morals. It reminded her of her dad and how justice and seeking truth were ideals to strive toward, especially when it was for someone you loved or cared about, and one thing was for sure. Her dad loved this city just like Gabriel did. She looked up at the ceiling, wondering if anyone was watching her and if her father or Jesus or whoever understood her decision to keep some information from The Seamstress to herself.

"God?" Simone beckoned to the empty room. Talking to someone she wasn't sure would even listen to a woman like her felt strange, but it reassured her in ways she didn't know how to express. "I don't know if You care, but keep them safe. And I really hope I did the right thing."

XDC

VII

THE FOG IS RISING

Marleen and Leroy rode in the back of a SWAT truck, sitting face to face, silently contemplating everything that had led them up to this point. The rest of the team seated around them loaded their MP5s and made sure their vests were on tight. Although it was safe to assume The Seamstress would have a butcher knife, Leroy understood the precautions. There was no way he'd let this maniac get out of here, but he hoped that the killer would live long enough to stand trial.

"You wanna know the weirdest part of all of this?" Marleen abruptly asked. Her straight, dark grey hair was pulled back in a bun, and he couldn't help but smile at how much she reminded him of Linda Hamilton.

"What's that?"

"This whole Seamstress thing made me crack open that dusty old Bible you let me borrow twenty years ago. Crazy how a mess like this really makes me want to be sure I'm all set, ya know."

"Of course," Leroy nodded.

"But I also have you to blame, Stone," Marleen said, punching his arm. "You make me wanna be better. A better cop, a better friend, a better person."

Leroy grabbed Marleen's hand and squeezed it with humility and gratitude. They both had been through so much, and it was high time they could be happy for a while. Together.

The van leaned into a halt, and the doors flung open, the afternoon sun beaming into the dimly lit truck. Six armored officers poured out the back door, followed swiftly by Leroy and Marleen. They parked about a quarter of a mile down Whirling Seed Drive so as not to provoke the killer into making a run for it.

"Alright, people," Marleen barked gruffly, "we are gonna have two teams of four. Stone and I are lead."

She pointed to the church. "The building is a one-story structure with a basement. I want Stone's team to check out the first floor and my team to check the basement. Stone, you lead your men through the front door, and my team will go through the back. If this guy gets to the back basement door, there's nothing but forest back there. We will lose him, so keep your eyes peeled. Shoot to wound if you can, but if he's running, shoot to kill."

The team began to march toward the remains of Holy Spirit Pentecostal Church, a place of worship now desecrated by a scoundrel who wished to defile the name of God and devour His creation. Both teams fanned out, Leroy's team heading left toward the front door and Marleen's team heading right toward the back door that led to the basement.

Leroy's heart raced. So many things were, at long last, happening. They were going to catch The Seamstress and Marleen had asked what he was always too afraid to. It was times like this that made him miss Jacob and how happy Jacob would have been if he had walked in on the two lovebirds in the precinct hallway. He couldn't believe that he mustered up the courage to kiss Marleen's cheek. Was going the next step really what she wanted? Should he have kissed her on the lips? Should he— Leroy shook the thoughts of teenage romance out of his head. Implementing a raid with your head a thousand miles away would always lead to someone getting hurt.

"Move," Leroy whispered. The team creeped in unison up the wooden staircase, hoping to avoid the broken and creaky boards. Two guys flanked Leroy on the left, and one flanked him on the right. The front door's squeaky hinges were rusted from lack of use in ten years, and its knob stuck for a moment before clicking out of place. As they entered into a small foyer, they were met with a plethora of obsolete greeting cards and Bibles that would probably crumble to dust at the gentlest touch.

The three men on Leroy's left broke off to check the men's and women's bathrooms, scanning every corner and giving a thumbs up to signify the coast was all clear.

Suddenly, the scream of an old man pierced the hushed ghost town of a lobby. Leroy burst into the sanctuary to find The Seamstress on the stage holding a bloody butcher knife in one hand and a human tongue leaking bright red blood like a faucet from hell in the other. His button eyes and bloody threaded smile stared directly at Leroy. Behind him was a writhing Wilford Hayfield.

"Freeze!" Leroy shouted. The SWAT team instinctively aimed their MP5s at The Seamstress. "You're under arrest!"

The Seamstress hurled the human tongue at them Instinctively, all the men dodged the severed body part. As they retracted, The Seamstress ran across the stage and into a back door leading to the basement, just barely evading the hail of bullets that chased him down.

"Marleen," Leroy barked over the walkie-talkie. "Shots fired. We have Wilford. The Seamstress is making a break for it through the basement. I repeat, the Seamstress is trying to run! It's all on your team now!"

Marleen and her team managed to bust the basement door open.

Sunlight was peeping in, but it was still extremely dark. All of the officers and Marleen flicked on their flashlights and descended into what felt like the belly of a beast. There were three rooms off a hallway and a staircase that led to the first floor on the left. All the SWAT team members filed inside one after the other, fanning off into separate room. Marleen walked down the hallway, gun in hand, ready to take on the world. She got halfway when she heard gunfire above. Leroy's voice screeched through the walkie talkie. The killer was making his way down here, and it was up to her team to stop him.

Out of nowhere, the back door from which they had come swiftly shut and locked. The only obstacle in the way of Marleen's team was a sadistic killer and pitch black darkness. "You should have let me enact my justice," a voice reverberated off the walls and curled around her ear. Male, late twenties, early thirties. Sounded caucasian. "Now my holy wrath turns toward you four," the killer growled.

Marleen saw an officer's flashlight beam in the farthest room sporadically bound around and then go out. She watched helplessly as each light in the next two respective rooms followed suit. When the light closest to her went out, she heard the unmistakable sound of a stainless steel knife ripping into skin. Marleen's ordinarily steady hand quivered like an earthquake, causing the glow of her flashlight to shake. She swore The Seamstress was upon her and fired two warning shots, the muzzle flash illuminating the whole room long enough to know he was not in her line of sight. Maintaining her cool, Marleen shuffled back to the door to see if she could escape without harm. Before she reached the exit, a strong resistance grappled her arm and jerked away her weapons. Her flashlight clattered to the floor, its light projecting a large shadow across the wall.

"If the reporter would have kept my secret," The Seamstress breathed into Marleen's ear, "you and your team would still be alive."

With those words, Marleen could feel the butcher knife sinking into her exposed neck, inviting the blood that resided there to run free. The killer flung her to the ground as she clutched at her throat and watched him skitter out the back of the basement and into the woods.

The ear splitting sound of two gunshots sent Leroy into a frenzy. "You three call an ambulance for Hayfield," Leroy barked, "I'm gonna go help the commissioner!"

Leroy barged into the basement, not bothering to check the corners with his flashlight. He cocked his loading mechanism in place, ready to blow away any demon or creature of the night he may encounter. He traipsed into the hallway of carnage. Three officers lay dead, one in each room, and in the middle of the hallway was a sputtering Marleen. Leroy bolted toward her prone body, thankful to see she was still conscious. He could barely string a sentence together, tears cascading down his face.

"Marleen, it's-it's gonna be okay. J-just hold your hand right here." Leroy wailed into his walkie-talkie. "Commissioner wounded. I repeat,

Commissioner Stricker is wounded. Direct the EMTs down here upon their arrival!" Marleen's trembling bloody hand grasped at Leroy's face. He looked down to see her at peace with her situation. Her lips stretched and contorted, struggling to form words. "No, no, no. Don't speak. Help is on the way. Please, don't sp—"

"Shut up, S-tone," Marleen choked. Her command was faint, but Leroy knew that it had taken all the strength Marleen had left. He held her close as the blood trickled down her chest and onto the dirty, basement floor. "D-don-don't blame Ga-Garcia, for this," she coughed. "Go...and get the bastard." She forced a smile as more blood seeped out of the wound and pooled with her tears into a heartbreaking concoction on the floor. "Be...be happy, Daniel." With those final words, Marleen's hand slid down Leroy's right cheek, leaving a bloody, tear-soaked stain.

Marleen Stricker passed away in Leroy's arms, leaving the detective a broken shell of a man sobbing uncontrollably over the loss of good cops, the frustration that this case was far from over, and the possibility of a life with his best friend dashed over the jagged rocks of reality. *XO*

VIII

OLYMPICS OF TALKING

Simone sat in the clean, barren office alone with nothing but her thoughts and the ticking clock. It was already five in the evening, and there was no call, no text, no scrap of communication letting her know that The Seamstress had been captured and everyone had made it out okay. The immense weight of guilt pressed on Simone's shoulders, crushing her each time the minute hand crawled another half-inch. What if they were too late? What if The Seamstress was still out there? What if both Marleen and Leroy lay dying in a hole somewhere and Simone was sitting on her hands letting them bleed out into the dirt? What if—

Rapid vibrations had her scrambling toward her phone. It almost slipped out of her grasp like a bar of soap. She hurriedly pressed the answer button and shoved the phone against her cheek so quickly she probably bruised her temple in the process.

"Detective?" Simone shouted excitedly. What she heard in return was a guttural cackle that made her heart sink down into her lower intestines.

"You just couldn't keep your mouth shut," The Seamstress accused. "You just couldn't let the old man die. And now, instead of one, five died by my hand."

Simone's eyes brimmed with water. Five was a costly number that could have included her partners. "You're a monster."

"*A monster*?!?" The Seamstress yelled, offended that she would even dare use this word to describe him. "*You* had your chance to save your friend. *You* had your chance to see what it was like to experience *true*

51

justice against someone *you know deserves it*! Instead, you followed the sheep instead of the shepherd."

Simone laughed hysterically. "I guess I'm not cut out for the whole murder-people-I-don't-like schtick."

"No, no, you are more than capable. This is the second time your words took a life. The only difference is, this time, you were given a heads-up in advance. Find me, Jaws. Just do what sharks do. Follow the smell of blood."

The phone call ended, and a sweaty, blood-smeared Leroy walked past the office door. Simone grabbed her things and followed behind him through the precinct.

"Detective! Detective, what happened?" Simone called out as Leroy picked up the pace towards Marleen's office.

"Go away," Leroy snarled. He briskly continued down the hall, and Simone suddenly realized that Marleen was nowhere to be found.

"Where's the commissioner? And where's Hayfield?" Simone asked, fearing the worst.

"Gone." His statements were hard and swift.

Simone desperately sought an explanation, refusing to ease her interrogation. "Gone where?"

"Not doing this here here."

Simone began stomping, frustrated she had to play Twenty Questions with this man. "If not here, then when?"

Leroy stopped in his tracks, rotating on his heels to face Simone. He had held his tongue ever since she crashed into his life, but he was sick and tired of letting other people have the last word.

"Okay, fine! *Fine*! Let's do this now! *She's dead*! You hear me? *Dead*! She's dead, Hayfield is dead, and you knew something about what we were getting ourselves into! So go ahead and *explain yourself*!"

Simone was beside herself. Her mouth quivered with shock, sadness, and a bit of surprise. Nothing she could say would console Leroy's grief. No quick jab to distract, no funny story to quell tempers, nothing would fix this mess. "Th-the...I don't know...The Seamstress called me and g-gave me an impossible task," she whimpered. Bile rose in her throat.

Leroy immediately retorted, "Yeah? So *you* thought it was best to *lie* to us, *your team*, and let us walk into a trap *completely blind*?! *How could you do that to us*?! *To me*?! *To Marleen*?!"

Simone was speechless, but she continued to try. "I-I-I don't—"

"*No.* There is nothing you can say that will make this right," Leroy concluded. He finished his trek into Marleen's office and collapsed in her chair. *Marleen's* chair. Though his cheeks were drowned in tears and his voice cracked, Leroy attempted to hide his sadness. "It wasn't enough for you to take Jacob away from me. You had to take Marleen away from me, too."

Simone braced herself against the doorway under the weight of Leroy's painful truths, tears uncontrollably flowing down her face. The unspoken chasm between them, the result of Jacob Winter's demise, had finally swallowed them whole and in it stood Jacob Winter.

About five years ago, Jacob was arrested by his best friend for selling drugs he had stolen from the evidence locker at the precinct. Simone was eighteen years old and had recently started her career as an investigative reporter. She was given the opportunity to write a story about the Winter Narcotics scandal, and she was the first to print an exclusive this big for *The Trumpet*. She tore him limb from limb like she was God Himself enacting divine justice on the Winter family. It reached national recognition, and the press flocked around Jacob and his wife like buzzards around roadkill.

One day, on Jacob's birthday, his wife and Leroy found him hanging in his closet, and the note he had left explained that everything said by the press about him was too much to bear. He told Leroy not to take his death to heart, that it had nothing to do with him making an arrest. He also expressed, almost with humor, he should have known Leroy was too smart to be fooled by his best friend. Naturally, word got out about Jacob's suicide, Mrs. Winter left the city six months later, and Simone was forced to write puff pieces for the next three years of her career.

"Everything good I have is always tainted by you!" Leroy screamed, pointing a finger at Simone. "You took Jacob, you took this case, you took Marleen..." Leroy contemplated the statement that had just flown out of his mouth. His eyes widened at an earth-shattering realization. He only repeated one word. "You..."

Simone furrowed her eyebrows. "I what?"

"You. It's you. You wrote an article about every single victim. You-you're The Seamstress."

"What?!" Simone fired back. "Are you insane?"

"Maybe. Who even knows at this point? All I know is that the consistent variable in this case is you."

Simone was taken aback. "So The Seamstress killed Jacob then? Is that what you're telling me? Because, if so," she said, thrusting her arms toward Leroy, "you might as well throw the cuffs on now before I kill again."

Leroy chuckled. "You remind so much of Marleen. Maybe you aren't The Seamstress, but her death is on you. I only promised to work with you because she asked me to, and now she's gone. So you're gone, too. Dismissed."

"No, you can't do this!" Simone protested. "We are so close to—"

"I said *dismissed*," Leroy bellowed, rising out of Marleen's chair. "You are off the case! Now get out of my sight!"

Utterly speechless, Simone fled the precinct, devastated at all she had lost today on the back of one small choice.

Simone sat alone in her two-bedroom apartment staring at her cell phone. The number of times she had called Leroy was insurmountable. She could barely get past more than two rings before he sent her to voicemail. It had been three days since Marleen's death, and the only person who would speak to her was the sweet old receptionist at the precinct front desk, Cynthia. Cynthia would constantly patch Simone in, butLeroy would send her back to the front desk. All Cynthia could tell her was that Marleen's funeral would happen a week from tomorrow.

Calling into work day after day and lying about being sick so she could hunker down in her apartment, Simone tortured herself for not having the answers that Leroy needed in his time of despair. She felt sorry for herself, but she felt sorrier for him.

When she finally conceded to eat something besides a saltine cracker here and there, Simone found nothing in the fridge or freezer. She decided to head to the supermarket, and as she perused the aisles for something appetizing, she ran into Jackson Taylor. He was buying cheap junk food in bulk, but he seemed skinnier than usual. His hair was matted from a visible lack of showering. She chased him down but pivoted at the last second because she realized how bad she looked as well. She made a U-turn with her cart, but it was too late.

"Simone?" Jackson said, turning his head sideways.

Simone winced when she heard her name and turned around to see Jackson's look of confusion. "Hey, Jack."

"You look terrible. What's been going on?"

Any other day, Simone would have ripped him to shreds for a blunt comment like that, but she was too emotionally drained to say anything smart. "Just a lot with this case. A friend of mine died, and I could've—" Simone's eyes grew misty, and her voice trailed off into a whimper.

Jackson was torn between excusing himself and consoling her. He finally caved and put an arm around her shoulder. Simone was not sure if her tears increased from her guilt or from Jackson's lack of deodorant. "Hey, it's okay," he reassured. "I'm sure it's not your fault. And if it makes you feel any better, people die all the time." Simone scrunched her face in disgust but ignored her base instincts because, despite Jackson's indifference—and lack of decorum—when it came to comforting people, he did seem to care about her and her troubles. "What I mean is," Jackson continued, "just because things suck right now doesn't mean you can't do some good." He forced a smile.

"Thanks, *amigo*," Simone playfully mimicked, wiping her eyes.

Right after he removed his arm, Jackson disappeared into the supermarket without even saying goodbye. Simone hurriedly checked out and headed for the exit. Upon entering the parking lot, she heard an old man who had fallen begging for assistance.

"Excuse me," the old man called between grunts of irritation, "could you help me up?"

If this wasn't a sign that Jackson was right about doing some good, Simone wasn't sure what could be. Abandoning her cart, she rushed over to help, bringing a touch of light into her dark-filled world. She pulled the skinny man up with one arm, dusting off his clothes, and noticed a pair of sunglasses. "Here, you dropped these," she said, holding them out in front of him. When he didn't retrieve them, Simone immediately felt embarrassed. She was handing something to a blind man. Sensing her discomfort, he laughed, took the shades, and put them on before smoothing out his white beard.

"Why, thank you so much, darling," the man said as he stretched from the fall. "I think I'll survive. I'm a lot more resilient than I look."

"I'm glad I could be some help to you, sir," Simone replied, wishing she could have been of more assistance to Leroy.

"Are you alright, honey?" The man pursed his lips.

Simone shook any doubt or fear in her mind away as if the man could smell it on her. "Yeah, things have been a bit crazy at work, and I feel like any choice I make is the wrong one."

"I see," the man nodded. "Well, that's what makes a mighty fine story. Good and bad choices, they're still yours to make. Sometimes, when you have a problem, you take it and *punch it in the face!*" The man exclaimed, brandishing his pale fist like a weapon of mass destruction. "Remember that, will ya?" He smirked. Whipping out a collapsible cane from his back pocket, the man turned from Simone and strolled away The tapping of his cane faded more the farther he got. "Y'all have a good day now!" He hollered. Simone smiled as she snagged her cart and shoved the groceries in her trunk, the old man's wisdom swirling in her head.

Marleen Stricker's burial ceremony was held at Cedar Point Cemetery, about ten minutes from the precinct. Close to home. Just how she would like it. Her casket was adorned with red carnations and bright blue wolfsbane. She was surrounded by coworkers, city council members, friends, and acquaintances. Simone looked around while listening to the preacher read a biblical passage at all the people that Marleen had come into contact with over the years. Even Locklear showed up, probably only as a formality. She sat next to Gabriel, the only person with which she felt comfortable. Marleen had no living family members left, so Leroy was asked to sit in that specially reserved section. He was even given the honor of tossing a handful of soil onto the lowered casket. Once everyone had offered Leroy their condolences, only the detective remained to watch the casket disappear.

Simone shuffled twenty yards back and leaned her right shoulder against a large oak tree. She clutched at her heart, desperately wanting to comfort the old-timer, but she knew that seeing her face would only bring him more pain and heartache. Gabriel walked up behind her, placing a hand on her available shoulder. "How are you holding up, Jaws?"

"I just wish I could find the words to make it all better," Simone admitted, still staring at Leroy, "but I keep coming up empty."

"You don't have to say anything. Actions speak louder than any words you can conjure. Even you, kid." He tousled her hair, and she elbowed him in the side. They both chuckled as they walked to their cars.

"I'll see you at work, Gabe." Simone reached for the door of her Volvo.

"Uh, no, you won't." Gabriel shrugged.

"What? Why?"

"Did no one tell you? Locklear let me go."

"Oh, my God, Gabe. I'm so sorry. I know that *The Trumpet* was your baby."

"Ah, it's okay. I'm too good of a reporter for what he's trying to do anyway. I've always wanted to start working for myself. Now, I don't have a choice."

"Hey, good for you. You're a lot braver than I am."

"I already knew that. It's too bad that you're still gonna be working for him. I'm never going to get exclusives now. Unless you work for me."

"Mm, let's see how your little startup goes and I'll let you know. See you around, Gabe."

"See you, Simone."

As Gabriel stepped into his car, another query popped into her mind. "Hey, what about Jack? Did Locklear fire him, too?"

Gabriel rubbed his chin in thought. "Oh, Taylor!" His eyes widened with recollection. "Nah, he quit. Said he couldn't take working for a snake like Locklear. Between you and me, he wasn't a successful ad rep anyway. I tried to call him, but he kept dodging me. Why?"

"No reason. I was just worried about him."

"Well, you should check on him. He always liked you, ya know?"

"Yeah, yeah," Simone nodded. "I'll check you later, Gabe."

Simone turned over the ignition, still unsure what she should do next. She looked toward Marleen's grave one more time. Upon noticing that Leroy had left, she raced back out of her car and jogged over to the freshly-filled grave, the resting place of a woman who, despite her best efforts, decided to forgive Simone enough to allow her to work with one of the best detectives Little Heaven had ever seen. This woman had died because of Simone's words, because of her sin of omission.

The weight of condemnation was so heavy Simone prepared to sink into the ground and eternally sleep alongside Marleen. She began to sob as the cold rain fell atop her head. Once again, the words to fix what she broke did not come to her aid. Only a few short phrases rolled off her tongue, and all she could do was repeat them in between her bouts of sorrow. "I'm so sorry, Marleen. You didn't deserve this." After a few more apologies, Simone stood up straight and vigilantly expressed one last thought from her heart as if Marleen were standing next to her consoling her as tears fell down her cheeks. "I swear to you I'm gonna find this guy... with or without the detective. And I'm gonna bring him to justice."

CQN

IX

MORE THAN A FACE

Weeks went by, and The Seamstress stayed as silent as the mutilated bodies he had left in his wake. The LHPD had a mountain of suspects, from former members of the Holy Spirit Pentecostal Church and local business owners who had run-ins with Clarke Holt to the one hundred families left destitute by Ezra Wisneski. Nothing added up. Everyone had alibis, and there was no concrete evidence to build the case against a single soul. All the police had was a motive, and after the fiftieth innocent left the interrogation bay, Leroy was more than ready to let this case go cold. Maybe they spooked the killer at the church and, after he fled into the forest, he decided to hang up the knife and mask and reintegrate back into the fold of what minimal normal Little Heaven had left.

He was an Internet celebrity, The Seamstress. Both videos had hundreds of thousands of views, and the potential for millions was on the horizon. What was more harrowing than any act of violence that The Seamstress could enact, more hellish than any misuse of a Bible verse to justify murder were the comments on the videos. So many people idolized him for what he did, and many even agreed with them. Leroy took it upon himself to skim through and see if any leads could be achieved, but after an hour of scrolling, he was ready to turn off the Internet forever.

Leroy bore a hole in the floor of his new office. Marleen's office. He was given permission to use it while the investigation remained open, and they even offered him the role of Commissioner. He refused outright and told them to never ask him again. The case was too important to be muddled by something as frivolous as a promotion. Besides, who would do a better job than Marleen?

After completing his thirty-third lap around the room, Leroy slumped into his chair and reached for the worn, red leather-bound Bible he had swiped from Marleen's house. Every employee at the precinct had cleared his or her busy schedule to box everything up so Leroy wouldn't have to tackle it alone. The afternoon was full of tears, heavy sighs, and camaraderie. Many coworkers wanted to spend time with Leroy and tell him it was going to be alright, but they all feared their efforts would come up short and decided to leave him be.

As if the answers Leroy needed would be discovered between black and red lines, he opened the weighty tome and leafed through story after story written by men who probably had no inkling how important and influential their writing would become. His fingers ran over the words as he read the underlined section of the crucifixion story and thought about Marleen. Had she really cracked this open before she died? Would he get to see her again someday when his time came? The last words Marleen said to him reverberated in his mind. Be happy. Happiness, an emotion that he hadn't felt since he arrested Jacob. An emotion that felt as far away as he felt from his friends. With nowhere else to turn, he bowed his head and closed his eyes.

"God," Leroy began with a twinge of nervousness. "I don't know what to do. I'm lost, and I've never felt this alone. I need to find this killer, and I don't think I can do this on my own. If it is Your will, help me solve this case." He hesitated, already regretting his next statement. "Even if Garcia is Your way of helping me."

Feeling determined, he decided to reanalyze his evidence board. On it were a screenshot of The Seamstress, pictures of the three victims, and each location they were found. Hayfield was the only one who derailed the killer's signature kill. Considering he was caught in the act that time, The Seamstress's ritual had not been fulfilled, but Hayfield still died on the way to the hospital from blood loss. Regardless, the body count was seven when you counted Marleen and her team, and there wasn't a doubt in Leroy's mind that they deserved just as much justice as the crooked men. Under the photos of the corpse's locations were the perplexing phrases in dark red paint. The Seamstress had prepared a tableau for Hayfield in advance, and it was a fitting phrase when you considered his despicable attitude and language toward Simone and Leroy.

YOU BROOD OF VIPERS! HOW CAN YOU SPEAK GOOD, WHEN YOU ARE EVIL? FOR OUT OF THE ABUNDANCE OF THE HEART THE MOUTH SPEAKS!

Leroy studied the board, looking for some shred of a connection between the cases. However, the only affiliation he saw was the one he made himself: Simone Garcia. She wrote articles about all three men, and now all three men were dead. He would arrest her right now if there weren't so many questions. How did she beat them to the church? Was there an accomplice that made it look like the killer was there while she was with them? Why did she agree to work with the police if she was the killer all along? Shaking his head, he reached for the pushpin holding Simone's photo to the wall and pulled it down. He held it in his hand for a moment and then crumpled it into a ball and threw it into the trash.

He leaned on the desk, sighing deeply. Which doors needed to be kicked in to further this investigation? Which life path was he meant to take on this journey without his two best friends? Leroy picked up an old framed photo where he, Marleen, and Jacob all sat in their regular booth at Big Joe's Donuts. Fran, their usual waitress, took the photo for them. Leroy smiled sadly, chuckling at memories that felt more and more distant every day.

"Really wish you were here right now to help me with this case," Leroy whispered to the empty office space. "Both of you."

"How did you find me? Who sent you here?" Jackson spit rapid fire questions through a cracked apartment door catching Simone completely off guard. She was doing as Gabriel had suggested, looking into why Jackson quit without telling anyone but those who signed his paychecks. Several times, she had tried to call him, but he was ignoring her. Being an investigative reporter had its perks and provided all the necessary channels to locate this guy.

Simone had checked on his last reported residence, a cushy apartment off of Red Mint Drive, and found an eviction notice on his door. After hours of stalking the usual places, she finally spotted him buying groceries again and followed him all the way to Wisneski Lake Apartments, the most run-down and dirty complexes in the entire city. She had staked out in the parking lot, watching the man spill his boxes of Totino's pizza rolls halfway up the squeaky wooden staircase. He was cursed to climb up and down three flights every day.

While Jackson was juggling his bags and fidgeting for his keys, Simone had approached him, spooking him so badly that he slammed his rusty metal door in her face and left his can of Cheez Whiz high and dry on the dusty welcome mat. Giggling, Simone jacked the processed cheese to use as bait. He swung the door slightly ajar, extending a hand to grab the precious snack. Simone had then pulled back, in hopes of reeling Jackson out to talk to him. She had too many questions and not enough answers.

"Who sent me? Jack, it's just me. I wanted to check on you, jerk," she said, tossing him the Cheez Whiz. "Gabe told me you quit, and you didn't tell me. That hurts."

Jackson peeked out a bit farther. "Look, I'm sorry. It was a snap decision, and I didn't want you to talk me out of it."

"Okay, fair," Simone nodded. "But I wanna know why. Why move to a crappy Wisneski slum? There are better places than this that are just as cheap. Better yet, why quit in the first place?"

"It was getting too crazy with Locklear pushing me for more ads and how he was running the company. It can turn anyone into a lunatic. So I left."

"Yeah, but Gabe stayed even though he disagreed with Locklear's methods."

"And I heard *he* got canned. Look where it got him…" Jackson trailed off for a second then shook himself back to attention. "I don't wanna talk about Gabe right now. Listen to me. You gotta get yourself out of there."

"No way. *The Trumpet* is my home."

"It's changed, Simone. I can see that, and I was only there for a year. Nothing is how it was. And what I saw in the morgue—you gotta be careful."

"Why? What's in the morgue"

"You gotta watch your back. Everyone wears a mask, and what's underneath, even someone as intimidating as you wouldn't wanna see."

Simone felt more confused than before. His hair was disheveled, and he looked as if he hadn't slept since she last saw him. He hurriedly shut the door.

"I've probably said too much. Good luck out there! And stay out of the morgue!"

"Wait, why?!" Simone stumbled in the stairway as she rushed back to her car, her head swimming with bewilderment. What was going on at *The Trumpet*? Was Jackson talking about Locklear? And what on Earth was in the morgue?

It was late, and Simone knew she would not be bothered in the office. She rushed through the building, running straight to Jackson's old office. She knew the IT crew would be lazy about deleting all the files, and she had this one chance to see if her hunch was correct. Her thumb found the power button on Jackson's old computer before she could even sit down. An old version of Windows roared to life, and to her surprise, no password was required. She scanned his recent files, looking for documentation of his ad sales. No such luck. She then remembered that ad reps had to email their sales to the editor-in-chief, so she pulled up the web browser. It had stored login credentials for every site Jackson had used. All Simone had to do was pull up his inbox she narrow the search for his and Gabriel's exchanges.

To her surprise, Jackson had tried and failed to sell ads for HoltCo, Wisneski's campaign and apartments, and Eden's Branch Baptist Church, and he was told three times to never come back to their establishments ever again. Simone checked the date. It was October 20th, one month before Locklear had shown up and seized *The Trumpet*. Another email a month and a half after that detailed Jackson's complaints that each company had actually bought full-page ads in the paper but he didn't get any of the credit. Gabriel's response declared there was nothing he could do. The date on that email was the last time she saw Jackson in the office.

There was one more thing she needed to check: Gabriel's former office for the key to the morgue. It was Locklear's office now. She knew that he was the type to work late because he was always trying to find ways to make money for the paper. Maybe she could convince him that letting her have access was part of a plan to boost the company's economy. She barged in without knocking, hoping that Locklear wouldn't be too chatty.

"Hey, sir. I was hoping I could borrow the—" The rest of Simone's sentence caught in her throat. Not only was Locklear here, but he was slumped over in his chair, his mouth dripping blood which pooled onto the desk and stained Gabe's ESV Bibles. The cuts were so vast that you could almost see his jawbones, but you could definitely identify a missing tongue without getting too close. His eyes were as wide as saucers, exactly like the ones of all the previous victims. She shook her head wildly. There was no way that this was another Seamstress murder. He had disappeared after the raid at the church. What was even harder to swallow was that Jackson, sweet, timid Jackson could be The Seamstress.

"No, there's no way. There's no way." She hurriedly flung the curtains open, hoping that whoever had done this was still jetting across the parking lot so she could identify who he was. Instead, she was greeted by the same blood red writing she'd encountered plenty of times before staring back at her, this time with a horrifying new message.

SO HE CAME NEAR WHERE I STOOD. AND WHEN HE CAME, I WAS FRIGHTENED AND FELL ON MY FACE.

Fearing that The Seamstress was in the building with her right now, Simone raced to shut and lock the office door. She pulled out her phone and furiously dialed the LHPD.

"Little Heaven Police Department," the receptionist answered. "How may I assist you?"

"Could you patch me through to Detective Stone, please?" Simone begged. "Could you tell him it's an emergency?"

"Of course, please hold."

The line tinkered a soft lullaby, and it was the only comfort Simone felt in the midst of this nightmare. Simone prayed that Leroy would actually answer this time. As the lullaby geared up to play for a third time, the line switched over to the dial tone.

"This is Detective Stone. Can I ask who is calling?"

"Leroy, i-it's me, Simone."

"What do you want?" He was immediately cold. She could tell that he was still mad, but there was no time for apologies.

"Micheal Locklear is dead," Simone sobbed.

"What?! Is it The Seamstress? Where are you?" His voice raised to alarm and protection.

"Yeah, it's him. I'm at *The Trumpet*. I was following up on a lead. I think I know who he is."

"Tell me, and we will go get him."

Simone felt the gravity of this moment. "Jackson Taylor. He lives at Wisneski Lake Apartments. Apartment 305."

"I'm on my way. I'll send a squad car over to you."

"This killing seems way more aggressive, Leroy. He may be going berserk. Don't go alo—" Leroy hung up before Simone could warn him, leaving her to fuss at the dead air.

Leroy sped through the sleepy evening streets of Little Heaven, and the white hot fire of vengeance filled his heart like a blacksmith's furnace. He knew exactly where the Wisneski Lake Apartments were as he and Jacob had busted their fair share of drug dealers and gangbangers there from time to time. All the instances they bagged a perp together, were called pigs together by people they went to high school with, all the stakeouts eating pretzels and talking about how they would move to Puerto Rico with their families and Marleen when they retired. All of those memories tied to one crappy apartment complex. Not one of those memories extinguished the flames in Leroy's spirit. In fact, they fueled it. Tonight, he stood alone against this insurmountable demon he was itching to stamp out with his right foot. It ended tonight one way or another.

Leroy switched off his police lights as he entered the complex so as not to attract attention. He snaked his way through the haphazard architecture and winding roads of the apartment complex then screeched to a halt at Apartment 305. Sliding out of the car was even a feat. Leroy gently pushed the door shut so the sound would not bounce between the buildings in the cul-de-sac. He approached the dimly lit stairway, pulling out his firearm and flashlight. As he drew closer to the apartment door, he noticed that it was hanging open. Someone had already been here.

Leroy entered the dank, smelly living room and scanned the quaint living quarters with his flashlight. Tinges of blue and red appeared in his sightline. Without thinking, Leroy opened fire twice and instantly regretted his decision. An all-too-familiar sound turned him pale as a ghost: lead bullets nuzzling their way into bare skin. Leroy fumbled for the light switch, towered over the slumped body of Jackson Taylor, and yanked off his cloth mask.

Repulsion ripped through Leroy like he himself had been hit with a lead bullet. Jackson had already been dead, his mouth sewn shut and eyes replaced with those haunting red and blue buttons. "We must be careful of the masks we choose, Detective Stone," the true killer declared, his voice rattling the fragile apartment walls. Leroy swiveled on his heel and pointed his weapon, ready to blow away...no, it couldn't be. Jackson Taylor was never The Seamstress. It was—

A dark cloth suddenly eclipsed Leroy's vision, and a pair of arms grappled him to his knees. He struggled and bucked against his hidden attacker's grip but could feel himself losing his own grip on consciousness. "For a mask is more than a face." Leroy wound his mind tightly around that last sentence, fighting to stay awake, but the cramped apartment grew darker and darker until pitch black was all the detective could see.

FXXMB

X

DISSEMBLE NO MORE

Simone clung to the corners of Micheal Locklear's office, desperately wishing she could tear her eyes away from the mutilated corpse. She looked back and forth from Locklear to the words on the window. The patrol car was taking its sweet time, so she occupied herself with a few specific questions. Why Locklear? Why was this killing so aggressive and personal? It was as if Jackson had his own sadistic plans for Locklear, as if he deserved a specific and more gruesome death than the first three victims. Even the verse was different. She repeated the phrase over and over again in her head. It sounded biblical, but she couldn't sure. *Gabe's ESV Bibles,* Simone remembered. She chose a bloodless copy, realizing she had never been this excited to read God's Word in her life.

When Simone was a child, she was often forced to repeat verses from the Bible just so she could sit down and eat dinner. Her mother took child rearing very seriously, but it got to the point where it was more about memorizing Scripture and less about changing Simone's heart. Religion had become her mom's coping mechanism after her husband died, but instead of using it to build a relationship with a higher being, she grew pharisaical and self-righteous.

Mother and daughter constantly fought about Simone's fiery attitude and unwillingness to submit to authority. "You are meant to be seen and not heard," Mrs. Garcia would scold. This relentless shaming and militance caused Simone to skip town when she was sixteen. She learned how to take care of herself and eventually got a job as a mailroom clerk at *The Trumpet*. She met Gabriel when her supervisor complained she undermined him when she was caught poking around the morgue.

Gabriel saw some spark in her, and he went on to teach her everything he knew about journalism. In turn, he reminded Simone so much of her father. Both men were known for dedication to justice and the greater good, and they each dubbed her with playful nicknames. Simone wondered if her father knew how bad his chiquita missed him being around.

Examining the concordance and the appendices was a larger undertaking than Simone imagined, but she found the verse she'd been hunting in Daniel 8:17. There it was, right there in black and white. Every word was a perfect match as if The Seamstress had copied it straight out of an ESV Bible.

Simone choked, her eyes widening with revelation. Every word, every phrase, it came from the ESV translation. *No, that's ridiculous.* She shook her head, the coincidence a fly buzzing around her face. Maybe this Bible was giving her some insight, but could the Holy Scriptures give her the clarity she needed so this whole situation would make even an ounce of sense? Her eyes then rested on a verse adjacent to the one written on the glass, and it was underlined in what she hoped was merely red ink. *"Gabriel, help this man understand the vision."*

Simone shook her head wildly, unwilling to accept these discoveries. She flipped to Exodus and compared the verse to the picture on her phone. It perfectly matched the one on the wall of the abandoned home. She slammed the book shut, and her world started spinning out of control. There was no way that Gabriel did this. Why? Why would he do this? And why did he torture her in such a way? The more she thought about it, the more it infuriated her. All the Bible verses he quoted, all the ways he was like her father. Did she really ever know the man at all?

She looked down at Locklear once again and realized that there was a key on a rope around his neck. The morgue key. Simone yanked it free, certain her father would be proud that she had unraveled a mystifying case of this caliber. What was left of Locklear lurched forward, lighting a firecracker under the reporter's feet. She zoomed down to the morgue, inserted the key, and gingerly creaked the door open. Squeaky metal steps trembled under her feet as she descended to another level. Illuminated by a single dim light were a video camera, a table, a chair, and the infamous red and blue button-eyed mask. Simone trudged through The Seamstress's studio and flipped the table in a rage, screaming with resentment. All this time, all this work, and The Seamstress was hiding two offices down from hers. It was her own boss all along. Her friend, her mentor, her father figure was nothing but a soulless monster who tortured and killed for his own malicious morality.

Simone's concern shifted to the detective. She had to warn him that he was after the wrong guy. As she placed the phone against her ear, a shiny object caught her gaze. Taped to the underside of the table she was a .357 Magnum pistol and a note.

For you, Jaws. Time to choose a side. -G

"Hello?" A raspy Leroy gagged through the phone.

"Leroy!" Simone yelled. "You're going after the wrong guy!"

"Oh, he already knows, Jaws." Another voice interrupted. Gabriel's voice. "He was just patiently waiting for you to put all the puzzle pieces together."

Simone balled her fists to keep her composure. "Where is he, you piece of—"

"Now, now, you will have plenty of time to fawn over your little Detective Stone, but now it's time for you to listen to me. I do not enjoy repeating myself, so pay close attention. 3478 White Lilac Drive. Be there within the hour or he dies. Bring the gun. You'll need it." Static bubbled up in Simone's ear. She pulled the gun off of the table and stomped up the stairs, praying for a safe conclusion.

Big Joe's Donuts sat at the crest of Lake Salvation, a rust-covered fossil that reminded Little Heaven of a better time, and Simone was ready to take back what this devil had stolen from her. She entered the enemy's camp, the barrel of the Magnum leading her steps like a holy shield beating back the darkness. As Simone marched past the plastic booths weathered by the passage of time, she thought of her father and their tradition. They would stop here every Sunday to get raspberry-filled jelly donuts and drink chocolate milk. He would always ask her what she wanted to be when she grew up. If you asked her then, she would have said she wanted to be like daddy, an officer of the law to help people like he did. When her daddy was found dead in his patrol car, a casualty of a gang war that happened ten years ago now, Simone was not sure what she wanted to be anymore, but she did know, however, that she wanted to fight against those who hurt good people like Esteban Garcia and her city.

If only you could see me now, dad, Simone thought to herself. As she moved deeper into the dilapidated donut shop, The Seamstress haughtily spouted a Scripture verse.

"But he said to me, 'Understand, O son of man, that the vision is for the time of the end.'"

Simone found Leroy tied up and beaten. Behind his left shoulder stood an overly enthused Gabriel. "Welcome," Gabriel beamed as if he had invited Simone over to dinner. "You found your way out of the labyrinth. Now it's time to slay the minotaur."

Simone pointed the gun at Gabriel. "You monster. You killed all those people just to get me here? For what?"

Gabriel chuckled and shook his head. "Pride does not look good on you, Garcia. I didn't kill these men *for you*. I killed them because they provoked it. They used their power to lie and cheat and steal and destroy. I used the very weapons they brandished to deliver the true justice that you know they deserved."

Simone could not believe the man she had regarded as her mentor was spewing this filth. "Even Locklear?"

"Locklear was a...special circumstance. I wanted to make sure his death was worse than the rest. Not only did he take *The Trumpet* from me, but he bore the mask of my old best friend. So I removed it."

"But who are you to say they're guilty? They could have been innocent for all you knew."

"Innocent for all I knew?!" Gabriel seethed. His knife danced and twirled in his hands. "Since when did that stop you from writing scathing articles about men who deserved to be crucified by the media? When did that stop you from saying that Jacob Winter was a putrid slug who wore a deformed mask of justice? To people like you and me, *there are no innocents!*"

"Why don't you shut up, ya crackpot super villain?" Leroy wheezed. "That Taylor kid was innocent, and you killed him for nothing." Simone clenched her teeth, fresh, hot tears rolling down her cheeks. Locating Jackson for selfish purposes had led this ravenous wolf right to his scent.

Gabriel stabbed Leroy in the leg for his insolent backtalk and sliced to maximize the oozing of the blood. Leroy winced, but his cries of pain were drowned by Gabriel's thunderous voice. "And I don't know about you, Simone, but even poor, simple Detective Stone has read a comment or two. Everyone in Little Heaven and people outside of the city limits alike agree with what I have done. They deserved to die. I am simply doing the world a favor."

Simone loaded the gun with a resounding click. "So would I if I blew your head off right now. For Jackson and for Marleen!" Gabriel began to laugh at the steely violent gaze in her eyes.

"I don't think you want that. I think you want to join me."

"Why would I want that? Because we are the same?"

"Exactly!" Gabriel yelled, ecstatic that his plan was all coming together. "Think about your past. A dead loving father. A religious and fundamentalist mother who abused you into repeating the Word of God before you ate breakfast. What was the first thing I told you when we met Simone?"

"That there was a little bit of you in me."

"*Yes!* My parents died when I was young, and my grandmother took me in. She was kind at first, and she even taught me how to sew. But as she got older, every time I did something wrong, she would beat me over and over again with one wire hanger in each hand. She would make me repeat something that I would never forget. 'Speak no evil, do no evil. Speak no evil, do no evil.'"

Simone softened a bit, almost empathizing that the scary monster was just as broken and afraid as she was. "Gabe, I'm so sorry. No one should ever go through something like that."

"But *we* did, and it was for *this* purpose. I realized that God wanted me to punish those who used their words for evil. Starting with my old grandmother. I smothered her with a pillow she made for me on my thirteenth birthday, and after that, I knew I'd found my calling."

"And you want me to join you because we have the same tragic backstories?" Simone gawked.

"Your struggle for the truth is how I knew you and I were one and the same. Your dedication to shooting at the evil men of Little Heaven's feet to keep them dancing inspired me. I created my own mask of justice to purge this city of the malignant tumors that decorate its very soul." Gabriel reeled himself back in realizing he was getting far too ahead of himself. "I want to travel across the rest of the state and the rest of the country and the rest of the *world* with you at my side, inciting true justice. But I know you cannot do that with one lingering tether to the world of these men." He then pulled out a small pistol and aimed it at Leroy's head. "It's time to decide, Jaws."

Simone shivered. In a frenzy, she aimed her own gun at Gabriel. "*No.* Don't you dare. Leave him alone. *Leave him out of this!*"

"One day, you will look back at this moment and either experience jubilation or remorse and sorrow. This pistol is on a hair trigger. You shoot me and the detective dies with me. However, you kill the detective in any way you see fit and I do nothing. We walk out of here together as a team and bring true justice to a world that is far past overdue for it." He lifted his free hand as if offering Simone a tangible choice. "Choose your fate."

Simone's gun shook. She paced in a small circle, weighing this impossible task. What would Jesus do? What would Leroy do? What would her father do?

"It's okay, kid," a ragged Leroy determined. "I know what's in your heart." He winked at her and closed his eyes.

"*Choose!*" Gabriel shouted, pressing the barrel of the gun into Leroy's bruised temple. "*What are you, Jaws*?! Are you a sheep, or are you a shark?"

Simone took a deep breath, closing her eyes. She extended her arms, aimed directly for Leroy's chest, and squeezed the trigger. Gabriel guffawed, amazed at Simone's swift bravery. She fired her pistol two more times, and Leroy sagged.

"*Oh, my God!* Yes! I knew you were going to make the right choice," Gabriel squealed with delight.

Simone knelt beside Leroy's body to untie his arms and lay him on his back. Gabriel's arm snaked around Simone's left shoulder as he led her out of the donut shop. "Come with me. Our mission begins tonight."

Simone silently sat in the front passenger's seat of Gabriel's red Volkswagen, clutching her gun like a security blanket as he pulled away from the donut shop. Tears stained her cheeks, and her breathing grew heavy. Someone as sweet and innocent as Jackson Taylor was taken from this earth all because of her dedication to the truth. Gabriel clicked on the radio, jolting her from her reverie.

"I am so proud of you, kid. There is no one I would rather be bringing justice to the world with than you."

It was nighttime, and the full moon reflected off of the dark waters of Lake Salvation. Simone remembered that, in the springtime, the city planted chrysanthemums and daffodils.

"Hey, take the bridge," Simone instructed. "LHPD is that way."

"Oh, you are correct." Gabriel confirmed, taking a left toward the bridge. "Can I be honest with you about something?"

"What?"

"I honestly cannot believe you thought that idiot Taylor boy was capable of doing what I did." He stifled laughter. "Now the LHPD thinks that *he is me!* Even though I killed him, of course. Oh, well, he knew too much anyway!"

Gabriel shrugged his shoulders and returned his focus to the road ahead. Simone rolled down her window and saw the murky waters of the lake come into full view. She smelled the moisture in the air, and she thought about the time Jackson took her on what he called a "platonic picnic" to Lake Salvation after a bad run in she had with Locklear. He was a genuinely good soul, and she would never get to see him again. She wondered if she would be able to see her reflection even in the darkness, provided she was much closer. She thought about her dad and, if there were a heaven, how happy she would be if she could see him again one more time. *Good and bad choices.* She recalled the words of the old man she had encountered at the grocery store. *They're still yours to make.*

Simone steadied her nerves, slammed the grip of the pistol into Gabriel's face, and jerked the steering wheel with all her might. The Volkswagen took a nosedive into Lake Salvation. She desperately tried to unbuckle her seatbelt but, instead, opted to slide out from underneath. She swam through her open passenger door window, but her foot was caught by her seatbelt. She struggled to swim up as the weight of the vehicle pulled her down. From here, she could see the glow of the moon, and it was getting darker and father away as she drifted into the deep. She closed her eyes, praying to a God she thought had long abandoned her, asking Him if she could see her father again when she died. Another object broke the surface of the dark waters, and she looked up to see the silhouette of a man swimming toward her. Was it God, her father? Some angel or reaper to usher her to the other side? Simone began to slip out of consciousness. She didn't care if what awaited her was salvation or damnation.

"Garcia! Garcia, can you hear me?" Simone jerked awake, the sky coming back into view. She coughed out lake water, spraying it all over one Detective Leroy Stone. He was alive and well. She smiled at him and wrapped her arms around his neck. They both cried as they held each other and gasped the fresh air of freedom.

"Glad you got my secret message about the body armor," Leroy mused, pulling Simone to her feet.

"I'm glad you decided not to go in all guns a-blazing like I thought you would."

"I almost did, but like Marleen said, what I say and do matters, and I am not ready to just give up and die."

Simone's happy face transformed to regret and sadness. "I'm so sorry about Marleen."

"It's okay. Part of me thinks she wanted to go out doing what's best for the city," Leroy explained. "I, um, I'm s-sorry for what I said when she died."

"No, no, Leroy—"

"My friends call me Daniel," Leroy smirked.

"Daniel," Simone inhaled, "you had every right to say what you did. I should have listened to you and been more professional about this case."

"But look at us now," Leroy countered, extending his arms. "We did it. We stopped The Seamstress. *You* stopped The Seamstress."

"*We* stopped The Seamstress," Simone corrected.

Leroy picked up Simone's arm and draped it over his, transferring her weight to himself. "Let's get out of here, young lady."

The next twenty-four hours were full of answering questions, sleeping in office chairs, and strange news. Simone talked to at least five different detectives about the incident at Big Joe's Donuts. Leroy was there to corroborate the entire story, especially after a couple of the detectives got a bit too carried away when she relayed the part where she shot Leroy. He was more like a father to her than Gabriel ever had been, and it took facing a killer for her to realize that.

Simone and Leroy were informed that Gabriel's Volkswagen had been fished out of Lake Salvation hours after the partners left the scene, but there was no body recovered. The detectives responsible for the retrieval reassured them there was nothing to worry about, saying that his body was more than likely at the bottom of the lake.

Simone sat alone in the office where she, Leroy, and Marleen had discussed the case. She stared at her gun, which had also been retrieved by the police. Leroy knocked on the glass door and presented her with some food.

"I'm sure you must be starving," Leroy said, handing her a burger.

"Definitely," she conceded, taking the sandwich from his hand. "So have they found anything?"

"Well, no. But I'm sure, if you clocked him good enough, there's no way he made it out. I feel like I can safely say that Gabriel is dead."

"But what if he isn't? What if he comes back?" Simone inched to the edge of her seat.

"We just have to have faith that it's over, Simone."

"Okay, yeah. You're right." She relaxed once more.

They ate silently, two people who could not be more different that were now alike in many ways. Leroy swallowed, pointing to Simone. "So are you going to still work at *The Trumpet*?"

"Absolutely. They need an editor-in-chief now more than ever. I think they're gonna offer it to me."

"I can definitely see you doing that," Leroy nodded with pride. "Are you going to write a story about this?"

"Um, I don't know," Simone shrugged. "Why?"

"Well I figure a truth-seeker like you would want the real story out there. Most people at the precinct still think it's your friend Jackson Taylor. You're not gonna let them believe that, right?"

Simone didn't respond and, instead, shoved her mouth full of food and looked away from Leroy's gaze.

"Simone, you're going to tell them who The Seamstress was, right?"

"I don't know if it's that simple."

Leroy stood up and took a lap around the office, soaking in Simone's words. "What are you saying?"

"What I am saying is *The Trumpet* can finally be a paper that writes truth without brutality, but if we tell the city who The Seamstress was, there's no telling if anyone will ever listen to us again. Not to mention all of those people who would lose their jobs if this came out."

"So the first thing you do as editor-in-chief is cover up the sins of the last?"

"It isn't ideal, no, but I would need you to help me do it if that's what I decided."

"Simone," Leroy prodded, "you know that this is wrong. Lying to the whole city, telling them Jackson Taylor did it, it can't go well. Someone always finds the truth."

"I know, Daniel," Simone agreed. "But right now, we have to think about what is best for the largest number of people and the city as a whole."

"The truth is what's best for the city! What about Jackson? Does he deserve to have his life desecrated?" Leroy yelled.

"I don't know. I have seen how horrible a truth like this can make things. What if the city finds out what Gabe did? Especially the ones who agreed with him? Gabe was the face of *The Trumpet*."

Leroy sighed and placed his hand on Simone's right shoulder. "I know what I would do, but I trust your heart, kid. Whatever you choose, you and I will see it through one hundred percent. I will be there for you no matter the consequences."

Simone jumped up and hugged Leroy. He embraced her, happy that they were both alive to have this conversation in the first place. She sat down and pulled her laptop close. Leroy decided to leave Simone to her work, but before he could get a foot out the door, Simone stopped him. "What do you think Marleen would do?" She asked.

Leroy smiled widely, shaking his head. "She would do what her heart told her."

Simone nodded, hearing her own heart clearly for the first time since her father died. She began to transcribe the story of The Seamstress, how he was hurt by the world and wanted to take back power by punishing those he felt were wrong. She told the tale of a loud-mouthed investigative reporter and a quiet old detective who had experienced their own traumas yet chose to fight for justice the right way by setting aside their differences to defeat a madman who wanted those who had sinned with their lips to fear saying his name.

LQDLTUNQNJMB

AFTERWORD

Howdy-doo once more, Dear Reader! I hope you don't think your experience with this story is over. I also am hoping you're not one of those weirdos that just straight up ignores a whole afterword. I took the time to write it, so you should read it, dang it.

Anyway, did you find it?

Did you find the secret?

I can tell by the look of confusion on your face that you have no idea what I am talking about. Well, it looks like this old book won't be thrown back on your shelf to collect dust like a copy of *Fifty Shades of Grey* in a Catholic school library. I told you to pay attention to everything.

Go back.

Find the secret.

When you do, you'll know what comes next.

Well, I gotta run. I got a nice lady coming over, and I'm making my special enchilada casserole for her, and no, you can't have the secret recipe to it. Anyway, see you in the next book!

Y'all have a good day now!

Grant Griffin

CPSIA information can be obtained
at www.ICGtesting.com
Printed in the USA
BVHW080931170920
588934BV00005B/487

9 781663 206374